THE UNDEAD

On the lonely moor stood five ancient headstones, where a church pointed a spectral finger at the sky. There were those who'd been buried there for three centuries, people who had mingled with inexplicable things of the Dark. People like the de Ruys family, the last of whom had died three hundred years ago leaving the manor house deserted. Until Angela de Ruys came from America, claiming to be a descendant of the old family. Then the horror began . . .

JOHN GLASBY

THE UNDEAD

Complete and Unabridged

LINFORD
Leicester

First published in Great Britain

First Linford Edition
published 2008

British Library CIP Data

Glasby, John S. (John Stephen)
The undead.—Large print ed.—
Linford mystery library
1. Horror tales
2. Large type books
I. Title
823.9′14 [F]

ISBN 978–1–84782–492–9

Published by
F. A. Thorpe (Publishing)
Anstey, Leicestershire

Set by Words & Graphics Ltd.
Anstey, Leicestershire
Printed and bound in Great Britain by
T. J. International Ltd., Padstow, Cornwall

This book is printed on acid-free paper

1

Disembodied Evil

They buried Andrew Pendrake on a cold, blustery Friday morning in early October.

It was in the little cemetery over three miles from the outskirts of the village, with the wind howling mournfully through the trees beneath an overcast sky. There were few mourners at the side of the grave. The tall, thin-faced priest stood at the head of the grave and spoke the words of the service slowly, but they were whipped away from his mouth by the cold wind that flapped and tore at his vestments. Strange, indefinable things, meaningless in that place which, for all its supposed hallowedness, seemed to possess an air of terror and evil.

This was a *feel*, something that seemed held imprisoned in the air of the graveyard. It was not because of anything which could be seen or heard or touched,

1

but something that could be imagined.

Five minutes later, the two gravediggers lowered the coffin on the canvas straps until it bumped and swayed into the earth and vanished from sight.

Fenner stood on the edge of the wet grass where it met the brown mud of the narrow, winding path and watched the scene with a kind of morbid fascination. He had seen it coming for close on three years now, which was as long as he had known Andrew Pendrake.

Why the devil had he persisted in living on at that place — even after he had been warned?

The old man had been cracking up for the past two and a half years. He, himself, had seen it coming. It had been inevitable, of course, that Pendrake should have died like this. What had come as a surprise, had been the fact that, in the face of the village talk, they had buried him in hallowed ground, with the priest to say a few words over him, even though his soul had been condemned to eternal damnation long ago. They even been forced to bring in a priest from

2

the town, twenty miles away, along the valley, to perform the service.

Dirt spattered on the lid of the coffin at the bottom of the hole. In the silence, it sounded oddly loud, like a fist battering against a wooden door.

Fenner turned his head slowly, glancing at the small crowd around the grave. There was Kennaway wrapped in a thick muffler and heavy coat, buttoned up high against the biting wind; Grosser, thick-set, turning to fat and shivering uncontrollably, looking as if he was ready for the last rites himself, and Susan and Bernard Brenson, standing silent in the drizzling rain, watching impassively because they thought it was their duty to be there when there were so few others.

Nobody knew whether Pendrake had any relatives still alive. Considering the fact that he was almost seventy, it seemed doubtful. The priest walked over and said something in a low tone to Kennaway and the two walked slowly away along the muddy path, through the rain, towards the two cars that waited near the foot of the low hill.

Fenner stood quite still for a moment, then turned on his heel and hurried down the path. The people there had seemed to possess an uneasiness about them which he had detected instantly, almost a suspicion of each other, seeming unnaturally quiet and withdrawn.

At the bottom of the slope, he caught up with Brenson. The other turned sharply, saw who it was, then gave a brief nod of his head.

'I think I know what it is you're going to say, Doc.' He pulled the collar of his greatcoat more tightly around his neck and tucked the ends of his muffler into his chest. 'You've been spoiling for this for a long time, haven't you? In fact, ever since you came to the district, when was it — almost three years ago.'

'Bernie — I don't want to argue with you, or with any of the others. But unless someone gets to the bottom of all this ignorance and foolish superstition that is rife in the village, there'll be more men — and women — going the same way as Pendrake. You must know, as well as I do, that there was nothing wrong with him, except that he would persist in staying at that place on the hill.'

'Has Grosser been saying anything to you?' queried the other sharply.

'Grosser? No — why should he have said anything? I gather from that remark that he's supposed to know a little more about this diabolical affair than anyone else.'

'No, no — not at all,' said the other hurriedly. 'Don't get me wrong. I realise that things have come to a head during the past few days.' He leaned forward conspiringly, and said thinly: 'Take my tip, Doctor, and leave well alone. Just confine yourself to treating the living patients in the village and forget the dead. Especially those buried on the hill.'

The second car moved forward slowly, stopped opposite them and the door was pushed open from inside. Fenner stood aside to allow the other to precede him. From behind them came the steady sound of falling dirt striking something hard and hollow. He shivered for a moment, then climbed into the back of the car. There had been something about

5

that sound which had sent an indefinable tingle coursing along his nerves. It had the ring of finality and aloneness to it that had seemed completely in keeping with the drizzling grey rain and the smooth stone crosses rising up out of the soft, muddy earth. The car started off after the other, the wheels throwing up gravel behind them. Moments later, they passed beneath the stone archway at the entrance to the cemetery, out on to the secondary road, turning sharply right towards the village, three miles away.

With a sigh, Fenner leaned back in his seat and tried to put his thoughts into some kind of order. He didn't want to think about these things, but as the doctor in the village, he considered it his duty to investigate anything that might have a bearing on the health of his patients, whether physical or mental.

West of the village of Mendringham, the hills climbed wild and stark against the lowering sky and Fenner knew from past experience that there were deep, dark valleys cut against the sides of those hills and thick woods haunted only by weasels and other predatory creatures, moving along pathways long untrodden by man. On the gentler slopes, out in the open, where the sunlight could penetrate, there were the scattered villages and isolated farmhouses.

But everything seemed to centre around the towering hill on the eastern approach to Mendringham. There had once been a wide, well-kept road running straight from the village, over the hill and down into Kenton, seven miles away to the east. But people had ceased to use that road more than half a century before, preferring the more circuitous route through the valley to the south.

Acting on impulse, John Fenner threw an apprehensive glance through the window of the car. Through the grey shadow of rain, he could just make out the dark, brooding shape of the hill, almost four miles away, but the visibility was so bad that he had to imagine, rather than see, the clustered ruins on the top, the remains of the once-stately home of the de Ruys.

He licked dry lips and looked away.

They weren't ruins, exactly, in the strict sense of the word. Rather, the house had been left to itself, to fall into disuse and disrepair, to brood and slumber fitfully with its fiendish memories and, if the talk of the villagers could be believed to relive some of those memories at times when the moon stood out silver against the eldritch clouds, storm-tossed by the howling wind which swept across the heath.

'Look, Doctor,' said Brenson, after a brief pause, 'you've been brooding on this thing for a long time now. Leave it alone, for God's sake, before it destroys you, as it did Pendrake.'

'It won't destroy me,' said Fenner confidently, but in spite of his tone, his face felt oddly cold. 'Can't you see that all of this is mere superstition? The de Ruys family is dead and gone. The last of them died centuries ago. How can they possibly be the cause of what has been happening lately?'

'You answer that one for us, doctor,' muttered Grosser, turning in the front seat and peering round at him, his eyes narrowed.

'Do you believe all of this nonsense too?'

'I believe that there's something there. I know what I've seen and heard, Fenner.' The other's face seemed to be twisted and distorted slightly as they passed under the branches of the long avenue of trees, and something flared briefly in the narrowed eyes.

Fenner shrugged. How many other villagers would be thinking along these lines, he wondered. How many nights had the lights been seen flickering among the tall pillars and broken windows of the de Ruys mansion? How many people, including himself, could possibly deny the existence of this *feel* of terror that hung over the village? He blinked and turned away from the others in the car. They drove around a bend in the road and there in front of them lay the village, perhaps half a hundred houses, if that clustered in the narrow fold of the valley.

The car stopped in front of the Royton Arms, the only Inn of which the village could boast. Getting out of the car he followed the others into the Inn. He was sweating a little although there was a cold nip in the air. For some odd reason, he could feel the hairs on the back of his neck begin to prickle. There was something here and in spite of Brenson's warning that he should leave it strictly alone and concentrate on his patients, he intended to find out more about it. To begin with, he ought to find out more about the de Ruys family who had lived in that manor on top of the hill. They were the basis of all the old rumours and legends in the village. That was undoubtedly where he would find some of the answers.

That was the trouble when you came to investigate anything like this. Rumours were vague and nebulous things, which had been twisted and distorted out of all recognition during the intervening centuries and seeking the grain of truth that lay at the bottom of all things, was like looking for the needle in the proverbial haystack.

Fenner shrugged off his heavy coat and went into the inner room where there was a warm fire burning in the hearth and everything seemed calm and sane.

'What do you think of Pendrake's death, Doctor Fenner?' asked Samuel Kennaway, moving closer to him near the blazing fire. 'Do you think there's anything at all in what the others say?'

'Nothing whatsoever,' declared Fenner emphatically. 'Just a lot of stupid, superstitious nonsense, the kind of talk I had thought would have died out of our society long before now.'

'But you can't deny that there was something — ah, odd — about the way he died. Can you be sure that it was natural causes? That he died of nothing more supernatural than old age?'

Fenner took the drink that was offered him, then said quietly: 'I can be sure of one thing, if nothing else. He didn't die from what the people in the village think. He was about seventy years of age. You can't expect a man like that, or any of us for that matter, to go on living forever. Besides, living in that deserted, broken-down place, must have affected his health. Damp and cold will have a disastrous effect on a healthy man, let

11

alone someone of his age and constitution.'

The other smiled slowly. 'You know the legends about the de Ruys family, I presume, Doctor Fenner?'

Fenner nodded. 'I've heard something of them. Frankly, I try to concentrate on factual things. I'm a doctor and above all, a practical man. I don't waste my time ghost-hunting. I leave that to others. But I must admit that there is a feel in this place. Not just in the cemetery this afternoon, although God knows that was bad enough. But down here in the village, I can sense it, feel it. A kind of coldness bordering on actual physical fear.'

'Still talking about Pendrake, Doctor?' Brenson butted in on their conversation. He looked to have drunk more than enough even in that short space of time. His face was flushed and there was a glazed look in his eyes. 'Mark my words, no good will come of probing into these things which don't concern you. God alone knows what that fool was doing up at that house all these years. Maybe he discovered a little too much, perhaps he even went the same, way as they did.'

'They?' queried Fenner harshly. He finished his drink and laid the empty glass down on the small table.

'The de Ruys family.' He hiccoughed, gulped down the remainder of his whisky, then went on thickly: 'I've lived here all of my life, Fenner. Call me one of the superstitious villagers if you like, a country yokel, but I was brought up with these tales. I went into that place when I was a boy and more foolhardy than I am now.'

'And you saw things, I suppose. Or heard them.'

'Both. But what's the use of telling them to you. You would only put them down to imagination.'

'It could have been that.'

'Maybe. Is that what you think it is?' asked the other pointedly.

'I really don't have any idea. And to tell you the truth, I hope to God that I never find out.'

Kennaway shook his head slowly. 'I think I'm beginning to understand you. Doctor,' he said slowly, taking up another glass. 'The scientific approach. That's what you call it, isn't it? You believe strictly in what you can see and measure, and unless you can take its pulse, then it doesn't exist. I'm not denying that it may be a very proper and convenient attitude to take, but don't you think it's a little narrow and biased?'

'It could be, I suppose, depending upon your particular viewpoint,' agreed the other quietly. 'Pendrake was fool-hardy, continuing to live in that place. In an atmosphere like that, I'm not surprised if the man went a little mad. It may be of interest to you, to know that I examined him thoroughly a little over a year ago. He had a weak heart. Any sudden shock would have been sufficient to kill him.'

Kennaway drained the rest of his whisky, his face tight, but composed. But there was something unpleasant hidden behind the almost perpetually frightened eyes. Something so unpleasant, that Fenner had the feeling that no matter how awful he guessed it to be, the reality would be even worse.

'If you want my advice. Doctor,' said

Brenson briefly, 'I'd take a walk along to see Chambers. He can tell you everything you need to know about the de Ruys family. He's made a special study of them for that book he's supposed to be writing. In fact, I think he came here for that specific purpose.'

Fenner was quiet for a moment. 'All right. I'll have a talk with him, if he'll see me. He's a pretty eccentric character at the best of times. Something of a recluse.'

'If you want to discuss the de Ruys manor and anything to do with the supernatural, he'll talk to you,' said Grosser heavily, coming up behind them. 'Another drink, Doctor?'

'No, thanks. I think I'd better be going. Being a doctor means there's bound to be someone needing me in a hurry, even in a place as small as this.'

'Sure, Doctor, sure. We understand.' The other nodded, raised his glass in mock salute and gave a brief nod of his head. His small eyes stared unblinkingly into Fenner's. 'But don't say that we didn't warn you. There's evil up there on that hill. Pendrake knew that, but he thought he was safe from it. If you want to know why, I'll tell you. Because he sold his soul to the Black Ones years ago.'

★ ★ ★

The other's words were still ringing in Fenner's ears as he left the Inn and turned along the narrow, twisting lane which led to the outskirts where his own house stood, set a little way back from the road. There was no sound now except for the thin moaning wail of the rising wind and the faint rustle of leaves, driven before it along the gutters. It was darker now and the clouds seemed to have become so low that he felt a strange sense of claustrophobia in his mind as he began to walk quickly through the slight fog that had formed during the past hour, rolling down the side of the hills and across the heath in the distance.

The countryside, just visible through the veiling mist bore a more sinister aspect than he had usually seen it even at night. The trees seemed larger than normal — although he put this down as a trick of the light and his overwrought imagination.

He shivered slightly and tightened the belt of his coat. There were a couple of street lights along the narrow lane with a blue halo surrounding each and the house fronts, dark and haunted, leered at him on either side, The pavement stretching away into the darkness, was empty and deserted. The only solid sound was that of his own footsteps on the pavement, echoing hollowly in the night. It was as if the whole village was completely deserted.

Pausing at the end of the street, where the last few houses stood gaunt and still against the mist-flecked sky, he looked about him a trifle apprehensively. In front of him, and a little to one side, the mist had unaccountably cleared.

Then he saw it quite clearly, standing out in perfect, grotesque detail. The hill was a black, shapeless mound in the dimness, with rocky crags visible near the top, and the awful shape of the de Ruys manor on the top, perched there like some crazy hat on a shapeless head.

Whoever had designed that place must have been a madman, he thought, shivering, with no flair for convention or beauty. It held a curiously haunting quality and yet there was something more besides. Something curiously black and unreal, fashioned out of shadow stuff which seemed to envelop it completely, not hiding the details as the mist would, but rather adding to them.

He needed sanity now, an outlook on this fiendish thing which could chase away the shadows and fears in his brain. He felt that there could be only one man who could do that for him. Reaching a sudden decision, he turned sharply on his heel and walked quickly along the way he had come.

He pressed the buzzer on Chambers's door and stood back a little way. There was a light in the window, showing behind the thick curtains, but several minutes passed before he heard the sound of footsteps approaching the door.

It opened a couple of inches on a chain and he could just make out Paul Chambers peering out at him.

'Who is it?'

'Hello. Paul. There's something I'd like to talk to you about if you don't mind. It's important.'

'Very well, Doctor. I suppose you'd better come inside.' The chain rattled and a moment later, the door swung creakingly open and he stepped inside. The door was closed behind him and he followed the other's slight, almost humped, figure along the wide hallway, into the living room. A fire was blazing in the hearth, giving out an air of warmth that touched him the moment he entered the room.

'Well, Doctor Fenner. What is it that is so important that it brings you around here at this time of night?'

Without preamble, Fenner said sharply: 'I've been told that you can tell me about the family who used to live in the manor out there.'

'The de Ruys family!' The old man suddenly stopped, looked at him oddly, then lowered himself into the chair in front of the fire and motioned Fenner into the other.

19

'Yes,' John Fenner nodded. He loosened the buttons of his coat as the heat from the fire penetrated into his numbed body. 'I know what the villagers are saying, especially since Pendrake's unfortunate death five days ago. I'm not interested in idle talk and fancies, Paul. I want to get at the truth. There's something here that is, well out of the ordinary. I'd like to know what it is and I think you can help me.'

The other smiled thinly. 'You seem to want to know quite a lot. Doctor. It may be, of course, that you're meddling in things which are no concern of yours.'

'I realise that.' He didn't look up. It was difficult to put his thoughts into words, but he blundered on swiftly. 'But if there is anything in this talk of disembodied evil, then I want to know about it. As the doctor, I consider that it's part of my duty to keep an eye open for anything like this.'

'I'll tell you everything I know, everything I've been able to discover about them, but I think you may be getting into something which may soon be well over your head.'

'I'll risk that.'

'Much of what you're going to hear, Doctor, may sound unbelievable. I thought so too in the beginning when I began my researches on the de Ruys family for my new book.

'There were five in the family over three hundred years ago. Henry de Ruys, his wife Emily and their three children, Martyn, James and Margaret. Some of the ancient records speak of a fourth son, Edmund, but all trace of him has been lost and it's generally regarded that there were only three, or that if there were four, Edmund died when very young.'

'Five of them. And they're all buried in the de Ruys cemetery on top of the hill?'

'That's correct.' The other rose and moved across to the bookshelf, slid aside the glass front and took down two thick, heavily-bound volumes which had an air of antiquity about them. Fenner guessed that they were originals.

Chambers's next words confirmed this. 'I know quite a lot of people who would give a fortune for these two volumes, Doctor. The original histories of the de

Ruys family, written in sixteen fifty-eight.'

He laid the second volume on the top of the table, tilted the lamp until the light fell full upon the stained vellum page, covered with the thin, almost spidery scrawl. Fenner bent forward, tried to make out the words, but even in the strong light, it was impossible. The hand was possibly perfectly legible, but the words were in a language he did not understand.

Chambers pulled up his chair, and turned over the pages slowly, finally pointing down at one of them.

'Here we are. The last of the de Ruys family. The great catastrophe which finally destroyed them but — but not what they stood for.'

'Go on,' said Fenner quietly, 'this is beginning to get interesting.'

'Henry de Ruys came of a long, unbroken line of knights and soldiers of fortune, who apparently came over with William the Conqueror in ten sixty-six. There was an old castle built on top of the hill some time during the twelfth century, but that was razed to the ground during the first half of the sixteenth century and the present manor was built over the site.'

'Do we know anything definite about these five people?'

'A little. It is difficult to differentiate between the truth and the myth that has grown up around them. The records of the time tell us that on his return from France in sixteen hundred and three, he married Emily Rochefort and they continued to live in the manor on the death of Henry's father, William.

'Their children were born during the six years which followed although we know of one, Elizabeth who died when she was less than one year old. The others, with the exception of Edmund, are well defined. We know quite a lot about them. None ever married, but continued to live almost in complete isolation at the manor.

'Then, in sixteen thirty-seven, something happened inside the family. From that time on, they became even more secluded. For more than a year at a time, they could have been dead, all of them, for all that the people in the village saw of them. No visitors, no excursions into the village as there had been in the past.

'But there were rumours of strange happenings at the manor. People spoke of seeing strange lights, of terrible screams in the middle of the night, of men who vanished and were never seen again, all in the vicinity of the manor

'Black Magic?'

'I fear so. Everything would seem to point to that. We know that such things were rife in England and Europe about that time. I know what you're going to ask. Why did they do it? I think the only answer I can give to that is — power.'

'Power?'

'It's something that happened in a great many cases among the superstitious people. Sell your soul to the devil, commit the most gruesome and diabolical crimes under the sun and you'll gain everything you wish. Of course the pay-off came once you died. That was understood. But even then, things didn't end completely.'

'I'm not sure I see what you're getting at.'

'Let me put it this way then. When you have some tremendously potent force, whether for good or evil acting in one place for several years, as it did here, it can under certain circumstances become a separate entity, divorced from all material and bodily things. As such, it can live on long after the man, or woman, who called it into being, died.'

Fenner shivered and hunched himself a little closer to the fire. 'You believe this?'

'I *have* to. All my life, I've gone out and lived among these things. I've seen and felt the terrors that exist just beyond the realms of imagination. These are eldritch things, ghastly things that throw a horrible, malefic light on the things that have been bubbling up inside mankind for five thousand years. Things brewing just under the surface of civilisation.'

'You sound like a disappointed man.'

The other smiled faintly, closed the book slowly. 'I am, in a way, I suppose. These are things best left alone, but I can't help wondering, you know. What black things exist up there on the top of that god-forsaken hill?'

2

The Shunned House

Fenner stirred restlessly in his bed, listening to the moaning of the wind around the side of the house, then reached for the lamp and clicked it on. It was almost three o'clock. He switched the light off again, leaned out and twitched the curtains aside across the window, peering out. It was a dark, wild night with thick clouds that scudded, wind-driven, over the yellow face of the moon. It was still fine, but there would be rain in a little while.

The stars were visible at intervals through breaks in the cloud and he could just make out the light from the solitary lamp visible in the distance from his window. The rest of the village lay in silence and darkness and the rising wind shook the windowpane and forced its way into the room as a chill draught through the space between the glass and the frame. The touch of the cold stream of air on his body made him shiver.

It was still autumn, but the wind was icily chill and the sound of it whistling around the house must have woken him — or had there been something else? He tried to think back to those few moments after he had woken, to pick out anything that could have jerked him out of sleep.

He thumped his pillow and sat up in bed, leaning his shoulders back on it, staring out through the window into the night. Nothing out there but the wind and the clouds and the impending rain. Or was there something more? Through a large break in the clouds, the moon had swum out into a clear patch of sky and by its yellow light, he could see, less than a mile away in the distance, the craggy outline of the hill and the gaunt manor perched on top of it. The cemetery where the last of the de Ruys family had been buried for the past three centuries, lay slightly to the right and a little further down on the far slope, out of sight from his window.

But it was the manor itself that attracted his attention. It was more than a trick of the flooding moonlight, it was more than his imagination; those faintly-seen, flickering lights at the back of the gaping, empty holes in the walls where the windows had once been. He sat bolt upright in the bed, his heart jumping.

Possibly, he tried to tell himself, it was an inevitable result of the strain and tension he had been through during the past two weeks when he had been attending Pendrake. Every day, until the old man had died, he had spent some hours at the deserted manor on top of the hill, deserted that was, apart from Pendrake himself, just in the land of the living, and those other things whose presence he had felt, and who were in that strange land of the undead.

The moon dimmed, went behind a cloud, and in the darkness which followed, he saw the light clearly, an evil, unwholesome, diseased thing which sent a tingle of terror coursing along his nerves, Sooner or later, he knew, he would have to go up there again, but this time alone.

He would like to talk with the priest, the man who had been there at Pendrake's funeral. *But I can't talk to him*, he thought, *because although he deals in this sort of thing, I doubt whether he'll believe a word of this.*

Terrible things had happened out there three centuries before. He felt convinced of that much. What they had been, no one would perhaps know. But it did seem feasible that Chambers was right when he had maintained that any potent force, whether for good or evil, might still linger behind in some strange and terrible, disembodied form, haunting the place where it was created, fed and nurtured.

How long he stood there, shivering, watching the flickering ghost-lights in the manor, it was impossible to estimate. The moon came out, shining through broken patches in the clouds, several times while he stood there, then the clouds swarmed over the sky completely, bringing the rain in glancing sheets. He saw the darker shadow, having no shape or form, but some odd substance, come creeping down out of the sky, enveloping the eerie greenish glow, submerging it entirely in blackness, deeper than that of the night behind it.

There was no further recurrence of the lights in the large, rambling building on top of the hill. The blackness was there and even in the occasional lightning flash that seared over the hill during the thunderstorm that followed, the walls of the building reared up stark and black.

He suddenly regretted that he had not asked Chambers a lot more important questions earlier that evening, while he had had the chance. Chambers was the man who could supply most of the answers, but he had the feeling that for the rest, he would have to go up there on to that black and wild hilltop and ask the questions himself.

He looked down at his watch lying on the small table. It was a little after four-fifteen. He made up his mind there and then that he would see Chambers and possibly Grosser or Kennaway and ask them to go with him to the manor and take a good look around the place. If there was anything there, it was a matter for the priest or the police, not just an ordinary doctor and a handful of the village folk.

★ ★ ★

'You've got some idea we might find something up there?' Grosser looked up at him curiously.

'Sufficient evidence to think that we're up against something evil and unwholesome. Something which may have to be exorcised if we find any positive evidence there.'

At the other side of the table, Kennaway rubbed the back of his hand across his chin. His voice was dubious as he said quietly: 'I don't know. I don't like to sound scared about anything like this, but maybe it wouldn't be wise to poke our noses into this business too far. What I'm trying to say is that Pendrake is dead. Whether he died of natural or unnatural causes is not for me to judge. But whatever it was, we can't bring him back, so why not leave well alone?'

'That's not only a negative, but a

downright dangerous attitude to take, isn't it,' said Fenner thinly. He drank his coffee and looked around the dining room of the Inn. The morning had dawned dark and cloudy, but the wind and rain had died away during the early hours although the trees in the small square still dripped water monotonously on to the ground below.

'Dangerous?' queried Kennaway. 'I don't see how you figure that.'

'Good God, man. Can't any of you see? I saw Pendrake before he died. In fact, I used to visit him every other day up at that accursed place. I've felt the evil that's there. Yes, even though I'm a doctor and supposed to think along strictly scientific lines, I've felt it.'

Beside him, Chambers leaned forward in his chair. The faint smile that had been on his lips a few moments before, had fled to be replaced by a look of slightly bewildered fear, a tightness that had spread itself over his features and into his eyes.

'Are you so sure of that, Doctor?'

'Of course I am,' snapped the other. He

spoke with the sharpness of irritation, trying to cover up the sensation of fear in his mind. 'Good God, we've all felt it at some time or other. Yesterday, in the cemetery, it was there. Every afternoon when I went up to see Pendrake, it was present, stronger and more malevolent. Grosser — you were there on three occasions that I know of, surely you must have felt it too?'

The fat man nodded his head slowly, the rolls of fat in his cheeks quivering slightly. 'I know what you mean, Doctor. I agree with you, but I still feel that it might be dangerous to probe any further now that Pendrake is dead.'

'Very well,' went on Fenner, his glance swept around the table, until it rested on Chambers. 'You're the man with the knowledge. Paul. What does it all mean?'

'I wish I could give you some kind of positive answer about that, John. You've been among us for the best part of three years. You know a little of the legends surrounding that place, and last night I tried to put you still further in the picture.' He smiled cautiously. 'There's one point which I did come across during my search through the old records. Something that has been worrying and puzzling me for some time.'

Kennaway looked curious. 'Like what?'

'Just this. If the records are right, the last of the de Ruys family died three centuries ago. But when the villagers burst into that place on a cold December morning in sixteen fifty-one, they found Henry de Ruys still alive. The others of the family were dead and whatever had killed them, it seemed to have been something not of this earth.'

'Go on,' prompted Fenner, as the other paused.

'The last words that old Henry de Ruys ever spoke were some kind of prophecy. He foretold that another de Ruys would come, back to the manor and that when this happened, all of the horror and the terror would once again be unleashed.'

'Another de Ruys! But that's impossible. If the last of this accursed family died over three hundred years ago, then there can be no more.'

'I know. That's what's worrying me.'

'Forget it, Paul. Come up with me to this place and see for yourself what it's like. For all the time you've been here, studying these old legends, you haven't set foot in that manor once.'

'I can't say I want to,' admitted the other heavily. He sipped his second cup of coffee slowly. His voice was low. 'If I had my own way, I suppose I'd back what Grosser said a moment ago. Leave well alone. Shun the place. But if you're determined to get to the bottom of it all, if you're still not certain as to how Pendrake died, then I'll come with you.'

'Now?' said Fenner tightly. 'This morning?'

The other shrugged. 'Very well, if you want to go right away. I've nothing else on at the moment.'

'My car's outside,' said Fenner thinly, rising slowly to his feet. He could feel the fear damming up inside him again. It was like being back in the cemetery once more, listening to the final, hollow thud of earth on the top of Pendrake's coffin.

Chambers scraped back his chair and got up. 'Let's go,' he said shortly. 'I'm not sure what it is you expect to find there, Doctor.'

'Neither am I. But whatever it is, the sooner we know about it, the better.'

The engine of the car whined and roared protestingly as they bumped and lurched over the stony highway which had once led over the hill to Kenton, but which had now degenerated into a roughly-hewn track, where the vegetation had taken a strong hold again. In places, the going had been reasonably smooth just outside the village, but now, as they approached the top of the hill, with the ugly ruins of the de Ruys manor looming over them like some gigantic creature poised on the top, the track, if such it could be called, had been virtually obliterated by the sprawling boulders washed down by the winter rains, and the encroaching bushes and roots.

Although it was late morning, the shadows were still there, among the tall trees which crowded thickly even on the higher slopes and the trunks seemed too thick and big for normal, healthy growth,

36

as if they were sucking something dark and poisonous from the ground. There was too much silence in them for Fenner's liking, and in spite of himself, his hands were clenched convulsively on the wheel of the car and he sat tautly rigid in the seat, peering straight ahead to where the manor lay, not once daring to look on either side.

Upon everything lay a curious sense of restlessness and oppression, a haze of the unreal and grotesque, as if something had been changed there, something which was not obvious at the first glance, but which became more and more noticeable as they approached the manor.

'Even now, in broad daylight, that place is enough to give me the shivers,' said Grosser. His deep voice rumbled from the depths of his massive chest and he sat huddled in his thick coat.

'And yet Pendrake chose to live here for more than fifteen years,' said Kennaway curiously. 'I wonder what it was that kept him here.'

'He was mad,' muttered Grosser thickly. 'He must have been. Nobody in

37

their right mind would have stayed here by choice.'

'I wish I could be sure of that,' said Fenner, turning the car sharply around the bend at the top of the hill. They were now on the same level as the manor itself. It stood in front of them on a wide plateau, the grounds overgrown with weeds where furtive, wild things rustled in the undergrowth. He stopped the car and switched off the engine.

Instantly, they were aware of the silence. It seemed to shriek at their ears far more loudly than any sound. An almost tangible thing, thick and heavy and oppressive.

Fenner felt the impact of it the moment he stepped out of the car and stood in the cold, misty air, looking about him.

'Nothing here,' said Grosser shortly. He turned slowly, peering in all directions. The look on his face was that of a man who expected something demoniacal and horrific to jump out at him at any moment.

'Let's go inside and get this over with,' suggested Chambers quietly. He started

for the door which stood g
open on rusted hinges. The
stretched across the stout wo
rusted, eaten away by the dull
covering of years. A tumble of brick
in the doorway and they stepped carefu
over them as they made their way inside.

The air in the wide hallway was musty
and possessed a strange odour that
caught at the back of their nostrils.

Kennaway was seized by a spasm of
uncontrollable coughing and the harsh,
dry sounds echoed and re-echoed around
the walls. The grey crust of scores of
untended years lay over everything and
their footfalls were oddly muffled in that
place.

'Hell — what a place!' muttered
Chambers. 'Being here, I'm glad I didn't
come before. I think it would have made
me change a few of the remarks I made in
my draft for the new book.'

'Forget the book for the moment and
let us have some of the benefit of your
knowledge on these subjects,' said Fenner
quietly. 'Can't you feel it already?'

'Feel what?'

t something about the
esn't it strike you that
han it ought normally
how light it was

ing to do with the
suggested the other.
little light in these
buildings at the best of times. I see that
part of the roof has fallen in. Only to be
expected, I suppose, after all these years.'

'This is where Pendrake stayed.' Fenner
reached the top of the wide, spiral
stairway and threw open one of the doors
at the top. They went inside the small
room.

It was quite dark inside for the window
was small, which was perhaps just as well
for there was no glass in it and the cold
air blew unhindered through it in an icy
blast. It was half-obscured by a crosswork
of thick wooden slats that had been
crudely nailed across it and Fenner could
make out little on the unswept, uncar-
peted floor. The stench inside was almost
beyond endurance, a cloying, sickly smell
that brought his stomach up in revolt.

Grosser wrinkled his nose and even Chambers took an involuntary step backward towards the half-open door.

'Nothing here,' said Fenner after a brief pause.

'Did you expect to find anything?' queried Grosser from the doorway.

'Not really, I suppose. But the *feel* is here.' He shivered. There was the sensation of eyes watching his back, but when he turned slowly, so as not to arouse any suspicion in the others, he could see nothing. Only the feeling persisted, growing stronger with every passing minute. He wanted to run out of that room, to dash down the creaking stairs, out through the splintered doorway into the clean, fresh air, back to the car. With an effort, he took a grip on himself, followed the others through the large, rambling house through all of the other rooms down into the cellars beneath where the musty, damp, choking stench was almost unbearable.

Then they came out at the back of house, stood among the weeds which had overgrown the gardens, forming a vast carpet of wild profusion which seemed to flourish even now, when most of the other plants in the village were dead.

'There,' said Kennaway suddenly, his voice tight. He pointed and Fenner followed the direction of his pointing finger.

The five crude headstones thrust themselves crookedly from the ground like teeth, worn and effaced by time stark and oddly unreal in the grey light. They went forward slowly, stood in front of them, peering down.

Chambers went down on one knee in front of the largest stone, leaned forward slightly, moved the loose soil, with his fingers as he tried to read the inscription that had been carved into the smooth stone.

Finally, he stood up. His face seemed a little whiter than before. He stood back a couple of paces before speaking in a hushed tone:

'So this is the last resting place of the de Ruys family. Somehow, I guessed it might be like this. An evil, out-of-the-way place. They'd never bury them in the hallowed ground of the cemetery down here. Not people like this who had sold their souls to the devil.'

Fenner stood quite still, looking about him, feeling that same morbid fascination he had felt when they had lowered the body of Pendrake into the soft earth on that rain-soaked afternoon. His palms felt damp and greasy.

'Let's get back,' Grosser spoke the words thinly, but his voice was rising swiftly in pitch as he stumbled away from the headstones towards the house. 'This place — this place — it's — '

Fenner could feel the hair begin to rise and prickle on the nape of his neck. He turned to follow Grosser, but the fat man had stopped only a few yards away, stopped dead, as if he had run up against an invisible wall.

Fenner meant to say: '*What the hell's the matter with you now, Grosser?*' But the words were never uttered.

Because then came terror. Then came fear.

Something was in the doorway of the house through which they had come a few moments earlier. A shadow-thing, without shape or form, or even substance. It was like a mist, dark and intangible, but gradually it began to build itself up into a shape. It gathered height and bulk and spread out into a form, and it seemed to possess a queer phosphorescent glow all its own that shone clearly in spite of the grey daylight.

Grosser was trembling. 'What the hell — ' he began, but the rest of his sentence never came.

It was a loathsome thing, seen indistinctly, but Fenner had the unshakable impression of a leering face that watched him intently, of malevolent, hate-filled eyes fixed on his so that he cold not look away no matter how hard he tried. The creature's dress was vaguely familiar. He placed it at about sixteenth or seventeenth century; dress such as one of the nobility would have worn.

Gradually the realisation came to him that this was one of the long-dead de Ruys family. He stood there rigid, unable to move a single muscle, numbed by the icy chill that seemed to radiate from the creature. A tiny pulse throbbed endlessly in his forehead and his legs seemed weak as water under him. The whole place reeked with the sweet cloying stench that he had noticed earlier inside the house. It was far stronger now and he could recognise it for what it was, although he had never experienced it before, having only heard of it from Paul Chambers — the abominable smell of embodied evil.

Out of the corner of his eye, Fenner was aware that the other two men, standing closer to the sunken graves, had turned and were staring, open-mouthed, at the abomination in the doorway. Then his gaze jerked back. He fancied that he could make out other shadows too, behind the first, lurking in the darkness which seemed to cling like an aura around the doorway. How many there were, he couldn't be sure. Perhaps his mind was playing tricks with him, he thought fiercely. Maybe this was nothing more than an hallucination brought on by the evil atmosphere of the place and his own overwrought imagination. But if it were merely an hallucination, then why were the others seeing it too?

Sweat popped out on his forehead and the horror of it suddenly washed over him afresh as the thin, sneering lips opened and the sardonic laugh that came bubbling out, floating eerily in the clinging silence, reached his ears.

He sensed, rather than saw, Chambers lunge forward, his face white and ashen, with something held tightly in his grip. Then he flung whatever it was towards the doorway, at the same time saying in a loud, but trembling voice: '*Fundamenta ejus in montibus sanctis!*'

The glittering object landed in the centre of the doorway. Its effect was instantaneous. There was a wild, rising scream of rage and pain, such as an animal might make if caught in the death-grip of quicksand. The figure which stood there began to fade progressively, sometimes surging back to semi-solidity, at others misting away altogether. It was as if two great and mighty forces were struggling for mastery in the doorway.

Then the blackness and the foulness

were gone, but the smell of evil still lingered for a long while, even as they walked slowly and hesitantly forward and Chambers bent to pick up the tiny golden crucifix on its slender chain.

'My God,' muttered Grosser thickly, having difficulty in finding his voice. 'We were lucky to get out of that. What in the name of heaven was it?'

'I think we have to admit that the doctor was right,' said Chambers slowly. He held the crucifix tightly in his right hand, as if expecting to have to use it again at any moment.

'Oh God, Oh God!' Kennaway was muttering the words over and over again.

Fenner walked over to him quickly where he leaned, sagging a little, against the side of the wall. 'Take it easy. It's gone now, whatever it was. And at least, we have some idea of what we're up against. I know what it feels like, but panic is no good. Just take a tight grip on yourself. Everything is going to be all right.'

Kennaway shook his head slowly, numbly. 'God, I never saw anything like that before.' Fenner watched him closely and waited for the spasm of fear to go away. When he was sure that it had subsided, he went back to the others, standing in front of the empty doorway.

Grosser was on the verge of breaking up too. His eyes were sunken in his fleshy features, his face a fine mesh of jumping nerves. He was shot to pieces, decided Fenner tightly, as if someone had taken all of the starch out of him, leaving him as a mass of nerves.

'I think we'd better get out of here while we still have the chance,' suggested Chambers thickly. 'After what I've just seen — after what we've all seen, for I think we saw the same thing — I don't believe it would be wise to remain here any longer. Not until we have some means of protection against the evil that is here.'

'Is there any protection?' queried Fenner.

The other nodded. 'There is, but it would take some little while to obtain it. And even then, I wouldn't like to be too sure. Evil has been frozen here. It's some form of timelessness that is bound up in this house, and more particularly out here in this unhallowed spot.' He jerked his thumb towards the graveyard at the rear of the house on the slope of the hill, where the crooked headstones glistened faintly in the grey light.

They went back to the car, bumped and lurched their way back down the hillside, following as closely as possible the course of the old road. For a long while, none of them spoke, all seemed to be completely engrossed in their own thoughts, trying to make sense out of what they had seen.

With the engine just ticking over, they moved slowly over the barren area between the rearing trees, dark and enigmatic.

Beside him, Chambers stirred uneasily, then threw him a swift sideways glance. 'You know, John, there's something here which worries me. I don't mean what we saw back there. That could have been purely a manifestation of evil. But hasn't it struck you as odd that this should happen after so many years when the house remained empty and deserted, shunned perhaps by the villagers, but without any hint of terror.'

'I'm not quite sure of what you're getting at?' Fenner looked at the other curiously for a moment, then turned back to his driving.

'Simply this. Apart from Pendrake, nobody has lived in that place for the past three hundred years. There have been records of evil happenings there, but all of that stopped, quite abruptly, it seems, over two hundred and fifty years ago. The place has been quiet during the whole of that time. Now, equally as suddenly it begins again. First Pendrake's death, and now this that we've seen today. Why?'

'Probably it's been there all the time, and with Pendrake's death, it's just become noticed again. You can live in the midst of something without really noticing it.'

'Perhaps.' The other compressed his lips. 'I don't think that's the answer. I've a feeling in my bones that there's something here which could mean more horror and terror.'

'What's troubling you, Paul?' asked

50

Grosser from the back seat. 'Something else on your mind?'

'I can't help thinking of that prophecy which Henry de Ruys was supposed to have made. That the reign of terror would begin again, when another of the family came to claim the manor.'

'But you know as well as I do, that this is impossible,' Fenner protested. 'If the family became extinct three centuries ago, how could there possibly be another de Ruys to take over the place?'

'I don't know. I only wish to God I did.' He closed his eyes and frowned in taut concentration as if trying to remember something. 'I think maybe there is something we've overlooked.'

'Don't the records show anything at all? Anything definite, I mean.'

'I told you, I've been through them all and there's nothing to indicate what he could possibly have meant by those words. They could have been the rambling of a madman on his deathbed. I wish I could be sure that's all they were.'

'It doesn't add up, does it?' said Grosser heavily.

Chambers shook his head, but said nothing further. They bumped the remaining two hundred yards to the bottom of the hill, then turned left on to the main road into the village. The remainder of the journey was accomplished more smoothly and after taking each of his companions back to their respective homes, Fenner drove straight to his surgery.

As he parked his car and locked the door behind him, he had the strange, tensed feeling that what had happened a little while before, would be only the beginning of something far more serious and nightmarish.

Perhaps there would be a little time in which to prepare to meet it, whatever it was, he thought vaguely, as he ran up the steps into his office. Perhaps they might still find out something before the inevitable happened.

But unknown to him, his world was due to fall apart into nightmare ruins within the next five minutes.

His nurse-cum-receptionist, Susan Paladine, glanced up as he entered. A look of relief flashed across her regular features.

'I'm glad you got back, Doctor,' she said hurriedly, 'I've been telephoning all over the place to try to locate you.'

'I was out — on business,' he finished lamely. 'There was no point in telling Susan what had happened. She might believe it she might not. But in any case it was something he didn't want to spread around the village; not at the moment, anyway.

'You've someone waiting to see you. I showed her into the waiting room.'

'A patient?'

'Well . . . not exactly. I'd say, off-hand, there was nothing whatever wrong with her. But she insisted on waiting to see you personally, so I suppose it must be something important.'

'All right. Show her into the surgery in five minutes. I'll be ready then.'

'Very good, Doctor.' Susan looked at him curiously for a moment as he crossed the room to the other door. 'Is there anything the matter, Doctor? You look as if you'd seen a ghost.'

'No . . . no, I'm perfectly all right. Just a little tired, that's all. I didn't sleep too well last night.'

'That's a funny thing for a doctor to say,' said Susan in a faintly bantering tone. 'Surely you could have prescribed a sedative for yourself.'

'Maybe. I just didn't bother, that's all.' He didn't feel in a bantering mood at that particular moment. 'Now, if you'll show this visitor into the surgery in five minutes.'

'Of course, Doctor.' Rebuffed, Susan spoke primly and went back to her desk.

Inside the surgery, Fenner could still feel some of the terror wash over him as he thought back to that incredible, uncanny moment when he had first seen that — creature — standing in the doorway of the de Ruys manor. A trick of his tired mind? Mass hallucination? It could, conceivably, have been any of those things. But there was more to it than that. It had affected senses other than that of sight. The smell of evil, and the feel, had been there too, something which he had been unable to shake off. And the fact that it had vanished with that shrill, high-pitched scream of rage when Chambers had flung that crucifix at it.

He bathed his face and hands at the sink, and sat down, trying to compose himself.

A moment later, there was a sharp knock on the door and as it opened, he saw the slender figure of the young woman who stood, a little hesitantly, he thought, behind Susan Paladine.

'Come inside, won't you,' he said pleasantly, indicating the chair in front of the desk. The girl came forward. He judged her to be in her early twenties, well dressed, with regular features. Not beautiful, but pretty and composed. Self-assured, he thought, but with a little uncertainty at the back of it all.

Susan closed the door and the girl lowered herself gracefully into the chair.

'I'm very grateful to you for seeing me like this, Doctor Fenner,' she said, and from the accent in her voice, he guessed that she was American. 'I'm in rather a spot, to tell you the truth and I thought you might be able to help me.'

'Naturally, I'll do everything I possibly

55

can,' he assured her. 'But why did you come to see me, Miss — '

She smiled winningly. 'De Ruys,' she said quietly, her words falling into the muffling silence in the room. 'Angela de Ruys!'

3

The Beginning of Terror

For a long moment, Fenner's blood froze in his veins, and there was a chaotic fury in his mind. He sagged a little in his chair and stared across at the girl's face, brain numbed, scarcely comprehending.

'De Ruys!'

'That's right. Angela de Ruys. Say, is there anything wrong, Doctor? If you'll forgive me for saying so, you don't look too good.'

'No, I'm quite all right. It's simply that your name came as something of a shock to me. There's — '

'I know,' she interrupted, leaning forward. 'A branch of my family used to live near here. That's why I came over to try to locate the place.'

He took a tight grip on himself. This was becoming more and more fantastic every minute. 'I understood that the last of the de Ruys family died several hundred years ago. That's why I was a little surprised when you mentioned your name.'

'I understand.' She nodded slowly, then said: 'Perhaps I'd better begin at the beginning.'

'Go on. This is beginning to interest me.'

'You've been doing some private research on your own?' she queried archly, raising one brow.

'Not exactly, but a friend of mine has for a book he's writing. I imagine he would be extremely interested to meet you. But we'll arrange that later.'

She nodded. 'I'm always interested in meeting anyone who is tracing back the history of my family, I did it myself back in the States. Unfortunately, the further I traced back the family tree, the more difficult it became to establish the truth. Beyond a couple of hundred years the references were extremely tenuous.'

'I can imagine that,' Fenner chose his words carefully. 'But you must have had some luck.'

The girl looked down, toying with her handbag, fumbling uneasily with the gold clasp. 'This may sound odd, what I'm going to say,' she went on. 'The name de Ruys is extremely old in New England where I come from. There seems to have been an origin about three hundred years ago. The date is a little obscure, but I think I've narrowed it down to either sixteen forty-eight or sixteen fifty.'

'What happened then?' asked Fenner tightly, speaking through clenched teeth.

'That was the beginning of the branch in America. It began with one of my ancestors — Edmund de Ruys who came over from — '

'Edmund de Ruys!' In spite of himself, he almost spat the words out. 'So that part of the legend was true, after all.'

'Legend? I don't understand. Is there something I ought to know?'

He licked his dry lips. 'I'm not sure whether or not I ought to tell you. After all, it is only legend. I don't want to fill your head with ridiculous notions on your first day here.'

Angela de Ruys looked pained. 'But

that's one of the reasons I came over here, Doctor. To find out everything I could about this branch of my family. That — and to claim the inheritance.'

Fenner felt the fear rising up in his mind again. Lots of little things were falling into place now, making a strange, bizarre kind of sense. He could feel his skin beginning to crawl as if a thousand insects were working their way across his flesh.

He realised suddenly that he must be making a fool of himself and closed his mouth with a snap. 'I'm sorry for staring at you like that, Miss de Ruys. But I must admit that this has come as something of a surprise to me. I don't know how to say this, but — well, about this inheritance. The de Ruys manor.'

'Yes, what about it. Doctor?'

'You can't live up there, you know.'

'But why not? I can establish my identity if it's that which is worrying you.'

'No, it's not that. It's . . . you've put me in quite a spot, Miss de Ruys.' He paused, then went on: 'You haven't seen the manor yet or you'd know how impossible it is. That old ruin hasn't been lived in for close on three centuries apart from a crazy old fellow named Pendrake who died a couple of days ago. You'd never be able to make it habitable again, no matter how hard you tried.'

'Oh, but surely it can't be as bad as that. If it's a matter of money, I think I ought to be able to take care of it. After all, I'm not exactly a pauper. Besides, I've quite made up my mind, and I think you ought to know by now that when a woman makes up her mind, particularly an American one, nothing in heaven or hell is going to stop her.'

'That's what I was afraid of,' muttered Fenner. 'I think before you make up your mind, you ought to have a word with this friend of mine, just so that you'll know what you're letting yourself in for.'

'You're being very mysterious, Doctor. You seem like a man with something on your mind. Won't you tell me what it is?'

'I think you'd better come with me,' he said quietly. 'This is something a little out of my province, especially after what I've seen today.'

'More mystery, Doctor.' She raised her brows again.

Fenner wetted his lips, then got heavily to his feet. 'We'll see Paul Chambers. When you've heard what he has to say, I think you may change your mind about taking over this place. In fact, I'm sure you will.'

She looked at him seriously, then rose to her feet and followed him to the door, walking through as he held it open for her.

'Susan, if there are any calls for me, I'll be with Mr. Chambers. Put them through there, would you?'

'Very well, Doctor.' Susan Paladine looked at them curiously, but said nothing.

Angela de Ruys was silent all the way to Chambers's house. Fenner guessed that she was turning over in her mind what he had said. It wouldn't be easy for her to understand, he reflected.

Chambers opened the door to them and glanced at Fenner in mild surprise.

'Well, I never expected to see you so soon, John. Come inside.'

He held the door open for them, then closed it gently behind them and ushered them into the front room. It was a cold afternoon and there was a fire, freshly lit, burning in the hearth. The room was warm and Fenner felt some of the warmth seep into him; and was glad of it.

'Paul, I want you to meet a newcomer to the village — Miss Angela de Ruys.'

For a long moment, there seemed to be neither sound nor movement in the room. Then Fenner was aware of the log on the fire spitting and cracking and of his own heart thumping wildly in his chest — of the girl's bewildered look and Paul's open-mouthed gaze.

Finally, the older man pulled himself together with an obvious effort. In the thick, frightened silence, his face seemed suddenly older than Fenner remembered.

'I'm afraid I don't understand,' he stammered finally. 'There must be some mistake. After all — '

The girl smiled as she seated herself in one of the chairs. 'I know precisely what you're going to say. Doctor Fenner was equally surprised. It seems that I'm descended from a forgotten branch of the family, from Edmund de Ruys, who emigrated to America in the middle seventeenth century.'

Chambers lowered himself into the chair near the long, oak table. He nodded his head very slowly. 'I should have known it, I suppose. The lost branch of the family. It all fits in. That's what Henry de Ruys meant when he said that another one would come to claim the inheritance.'

'And he was right,' said the girl brightly. 'That's exactly why I am here. I understand that the place will need some rebuilding and modernising, but I've got sufficient money for that. It's been my dream for as long as I can remember, to come back over here and take over the old family manor.'

Fenner glanced across at Chambers and saw the look on the other's face. The strained silence was broken finally by the girl as she said soberly: 'I think you'd better tell me everything, you know. After all, this is my concern and if there is anything I ought to know, then now is the time to give me it straight. If there are any snags I haven't considered, if the laws here are different from over in the States, then I — '

Chambers cleared his throat. 'I think you have a right to know, of course, Miss de Ruys, although I doubt whether you are going to believe what we have to tell you. You see, it all began with a man named Pendrake.'

'Yes, I remember the Doctor mentioning that name a little while ago.' The girl leaned forward and rested her chin on her hand.

'This man, Pendrake, stayed at the manor for the past five or six years. He was a recluse, eccentric and for the first three years or so, his wife lived there with him. They were ordinary, stolid people like ourselves in spite of this eccentricity of theirs for utter privacy.

'Then, in July, two years ago, the poor woman was found wandering on the hillside in a state of shock. She screamed aloud about things at the manor, things which she couldn't describe, but which were clearly sufficiently horrible or evil, to drive her out of her wits. In her ravings the doctor here will testify, there was only talk of things that moved or fluttered or came drifting in out of the dark. But always, they seemed to come from the rear of the house, from the place where the last of the family were buried.'

'Poor creature. What happened to her?'

'She had to be locked up for her own good. There was the fear that with her brain in that chaotic condition she might do harm to herself, or someone else. She died less than two months later never regaining her sanity. All the time, she was found to be crouched against the wall of her room, her arms raised as though to fend off something huge and grotesque which was menacing her and on her face was an expression of such horror that, pray God I never see the like of it again in my life.'

It was clear to Fenner that the story had had a subduing effect on the girl, but the look of determination and quiet confidence was still there on her face and in her eyes. She wasn't one of those kind who gave in as easily as all that, he reflected, and it was going to take more than a simple ghost story to dissuade her from her chosen course.

'Is that all that happened?' she asked finally.

Chambers shook his head, 'No — I only wish to God it were. But there was more to come. Pendrake, of course, refused go leave the place. It seemed to have gained such a hold on him that nothing would make him leave it, even when his health began to fail a few months ago.

'Doctor Fenner used to visit him regularly, but he grew steadily worse and when he died two days ago, I suppose it would normally have come as a relief to all of us who knew him. But the look on his face was so reminiscent of that on his wife's that Doctor Fenner had some qualms about signing the death certificate.'

'I see. No wonder the place has a bad reputation round these parts. But these were old people. Maybe their hearts weren't too sound. They could have died of shock from the smallest cause.'

'They could have,' conceded Fenner,

'but we believe that they didn't. Not in the way you mean. We went up there this morning, four of us, to take a look around. What we saw has convinced us that there is evil there. Pure, unadulterated evil.'

Angela de Ruys uttered a short nervous laugh. 'I thought nobody believed in such things these days. You can't be serious.'

'We're perfectly serious,' said Chambers gravely. 'We don't kid people about things like this, Miss de Ruys.'

'Then what did you see exactly?' It was a direct question and Fenner knew instinctively that there was no sense in beating about the bush.

'Call it a manifestation if you like but we all saw it. The shape of a man standing in the rear doorway of the manor. It wasn't that of any living man, I'm positive of that. So are Chambers and the other two men with us. And the aura of sheer evil which came from it was overpowering.'

'You mean it was a ghost?' The girl laughed again; a sharp, brittle sound. 'Maybe it was one of my ancestors come back to teach you all a lesson for disturbing him.'

Chambers said tightly: 'I wouldn't treat it as lightly as that, Miss de Ruys. Evil like this is no joke, I can assure you.' His face was covered with a light sheen of sweat that glistened in the light of the fire. 'I've studied these — phenomena — if you call them that for the best part of thirty years. There are Powers of Darkness in the world just as there are Powers of Light.

'After all, you wouldn't deny the miracles that have been performed in the past. Believe me, the force of evil is just as strong, just as potent if carried out in the hands of a skilled person.'

'And you think that something like that happened up there?'

'If the records are to be believed, the manor was used for some terrible purpose three centuries ago. The records only hint at what diabolical rites were performed, but it's relatively easy to conclude that they carried out the Black Mass, and possibly human sacrifice.'

The girl's eyes widened. She made to speak but the words seemed to stick in her throat and Chambers went on hurriedly: 'I know that must shock you and seem incredible, but nevertheless, I do assure you most sincerely that it's perfectly true. Official documents of that time show that almost a score of people vanished inexplicably near the manor in the space of three years. That seems too much of a coincidence for my way of thinking.

'I know what's running through your mind. Why on earth did they do such diabolical things?' He smiled thinly. 'In all of my researches, I've discovered that there are two main reasons for these fiendish practices. Power or immortality. In this case, I think it's fairly obvious that the de Ruys family had all the power they needed in the area.'

'So you think they were seeking after immortality,' said Fenner before the girl could speak. He felt a shiver go through him in spite of the warmth in the room.

'I not only think they sought immortality,' said Chambers slowly, 'but I believe that through these evil rites, they gained it — in a sense. Oh, they didn't live on and on as your usual concept of immortality would have had them do. They really did die, in a physical sense, all those years ago. But something of them, call it a *damned* soul, if you like, lived on in that place. Something which couldn't die and because it was spawned of evil, it *was* evil. Terrible and dangerous it was crystallised into that place, into those walls frozen there so that time made no difference. What we saw this morning, was a manifestation of that evil thing.'

'And that was the reason why it vanished when you threw that golden crucifix at it.'

'Exactly. We were lucky. The next time we may not be so fortunate. Because, believe me, this thing is far more dangerous than any living entity. It could destroy us completely and horribly in a single instant of time. That's why, Miss de Ruys, I beg of you to give up this idea of yours to modernise the manor and live in that accursed place.'

For a moment Fenner thought that the other had succeeded. There was a look of horror in the girl's eyes blending almost imperceptibly into one of indecision.

Then Angela de Ruys sat bolt upright in her chair, shaking her head emphatically. 'No, I'm damned if I'll give all this up just for a lot of superstitious nonsense. Ghost or no ghost, I intend to go through with my plans.'

Chambers heaved a heavy sigh. 'You're being extremely foolish. I only hope you live to regret it.'

She looked at him curiously. 'I caught a glimpse of the place on my way into the village. The taxi driver pointed it out to me. It looks old and a little forbidding, but kind of cute in spite of that. Maybe it's the grimness that gives it its peculiar charm. And once it's put back into some state of repair, I think even the grimness will change.

'And as for this hallucination you claim you saw — well, although I won't admit that it really was a physical manifestation as you seem convinced, has it ever struck you that it might have no wish to harm me. After all, I'm one of the family myself.'

'I'm afraid I haven't got an answer to

that one, Miss de Ruys. All that I can think of at the moment is what Henry de Ruys is reputed to have said when he was found dying by the villagers. That the evil of those days would return once again when a de Ruys came back to claim the inheritance. Apart from ourselves, and I trust we can think of ourselves as reasonable, logical people, what will the villagers think when they discover that the family didn't die out altogether three centuries ago?'

'That's no concern of mine, is it?' she said crisply, 'and if they won't help me to repair the place, if they're scared of it, well, I've thought of that too. I'll get some people I've heard of in the nearby town to do it. I'm sure they won't be bothered by any of these old superstitions so long as the money is good.'

'That's true,' Fenner agreed. 'But you will be in terrible danger if you go through with this.'

'I think you're only trying to frighten me for some reason known only to yourselves.' A quick frown clouded her face for a moment, then she got to her feet.

'I'm sorry you feel like that,' said Chambers softly, getting up. 'Perhaps you were right in thinking that no harm will come to another member of the family but wouldn't bank on that if I were you.'

'Is there an Inn anywhere in the village where I can put up?' She changed the subject adroitly. 'As I think I'll be staying here for quite some time, I think I'd better have a place to stay until I can move into the manor.'

'They'll take good care of you down at the Royton Arms,' said Fenner, following her to the door. 'I'll show you the way there.'

★　★　★

It was near dusk, the time of day when the whole earth seemed to stand still on the brink of silence, just before the night came. The pale wintry sun was sinking down behind the grotesque spectre of the old mansion on top of the hill. From his window, it looked quiet and innocent, standing out against the sky. He grimaced. Innocent? Quiet?

74

Mendringham, he thought fiercely, a little village with not too many houses along the single street and not too many people. A village with a terrible history. A quiet, picturesque little place that was only just beginning to realise that it had spawned five terrible monsters three centuries earlier.

He had supper and read for a while, trying to keep his mind off what was happening in the village. But the book failed to hold his interest and he soon threw it down in exasperation.

It was now almost three weeks since Angela de Ruys had come to Mendringham. Three weeks in which so much had happened. True to her promise, she had brought in contractors from the nearby town. She could afford to pay and throughout the short, wintry days, men had swarmed over the dilapidated, ruined manor, knocking down walls and partitions, and rebuilding them from the foundations, putting in windows, repairing the roof.

But it was significant that none of the men would work there, or even remain in the place, a single instant after the sun went down and the darkness of night came out of the east. There had been the strange accidents on the site too. Two men were already in hospital, severely injured after falling from scaffolding, falls that could not be satisfactorily explained.

Other men had spoken of cold, icy blasts of air that had swirled about them at inexplicable moments when there were no doors or windows open and everything else in the place had been still. Because of what he himself had seen, all of these queer happenings were fixed indelibly in his mind. By the end of the second week, the whole of Mendringham had heard of the strange happenings. People spoke in hushed whispers. Some even appeared to be openly antagonistic towards Angela de Ruys. You couldn't keep accidents like that hushed up in so small a place as Mendringham, even if you had as much money and determination as Angela de Ruys.

He had deliberately stayed away from the manor since the first meeting with Angela de Ruys, partly because of fear and partly because of his disapproval of what was being done. The feeling of impending disaster had been growing steadily during the past two weeks.

What new horror those diabolical creatures were preparing to unleash, he did not know, nor could he even begin to guess, nor could he know when it would strike. But when it came, he hoped to God that they would be prepared to meet it.

For several minutes before deciding to turn in, he glanced furtively through the window towards the looming, dark mass of the hill. Although the sun had already set, there was still sufficient light for him to be able to pick out most of the details.

The building had altered quite considerably during the past week or so. The workmen seemed to be working hurriedly as if anxious to get the job finished as quickly as possible and get away to some other work. The whole place seemed to lie in silence. Fenner's brief, intent anxiety began to fade a little.

There could be a logical explanation behind the accidents up there on the hill, but at the moment, he was damned if he could see it. For a tense moment, he toyed with the idea that Chambers had been wrong, that all of this talk and study had gone to his brain and he had somehow forced them to see that creature standing in the doorway. Mental suggestion, possibly innocently-induced hypnosis could be the explanation without Chambers even being aware of it.

He shook his head, rejecting the notion. That couldn't possibly explain that terrible scream of pain and anger that they had all heard when the crucifix had landed in the open doorway.

One thing was curious, though. Every night, for the past three weeks, he had stared out at the manor, watching for the slightest sign of the strange and eerie light he had seen some little time before, but it had never appeared again. Did that mean that the girl was right in her supposition that whatever it was which haunted that place it would do no harm to her — or was it that the incredible horrific thing, whatever it had been, had gone back to the place where it had been hidden away from the world for all these years, gone back to bide its time when it might come again.

Quite suddenly, he knew that he had to go back to that place if only to ease his mind and rid it of the loathsome thought and half-formed ideas which kept running through it, giving him little rest at night. But he would have to go when there was no one else there. During the daylight hours, with the workmen on the site, he would find nothing.

But at night, when there was a moon by which to see he might find something. But first, he would have a talk with Chambers. The old man was no fool and he would know best what protection was necessary.

The idea grew on him. He looked at his watch. It was barely eight-thirty. It wasn't too late in the evening. Although dark, he knew that Chambers would still be up. He swung his legs over the side of the bed and padded through into the other room, to the phone. The cold air inside the room sent chills over his body.

There was the familiar buzzing at the

other end of the line, then a sharp click and Paul Chambers's voice said: 'Hello?'

'Paul Fenner here. Sorry for disturbing you at this time of night, but there's something I have to talk to you about. It's important.'

'Anything to do with the de Ruys manor, John?'

'How did you guess?'

'Let's say I'm psychic and leave it at that, shall we?'

'O.K. When can I come over? Right away?'

'Certainly if it's as urgent as that. If you've something on your mind, better to get it off by talking with someone, otherwise you'll never get any sleep. You ought to know that, Doctor.'

'I'll be right over.' He replaced the phone in its cradle.

Ten minutes later, he was walking up the narrow, well-tended garden path towards the other's house. There was a light in the window as he closed the gate behind him, a flickering red light, which just showed behind the thin curtain. At least, the other had waited up for him, he thought, then stopped dead in his tracks.

Something showed behind the curtain, showed itself only for a brief instant, but even in that short space of time, he recognised that it was not Paul Chambers, nor anyone that even remotely resembled him. In fact, his mind screamed at him: it hadn't resembled a human being at all.

And the scream, when it came, ringing in his ears, was more of a shriek of terrible, inhuman fear, than an actual scream. Fenner felt a slight tingling in the air, quivering along the muscles of his body. The flickering lurid light was brighter now, stronger. And yet, there was no actual impression of fire, or warmth, behind it.

In spite of himself, he began to run, shouting the other's name at the top of his voice.

4

Something of the Dark

The scream was still ringing in his ears as he reached the door. He noticed that the lurid red glow had faded slightly behind the twitching curtains. Then as he reached the door and hammered loudly on it, the screams fell silent and there was no sound at all in the house. The sudden silence hit him like a physical blow. It was even more terrible than the scream of pure animal fear which had preceded it.

Wildly, he thrust at the door. It was locked. Stepping back, he flung his shoulder at it. The door was stout, strongly built, and he had to hurl the full weight of his athletic body at it several times before there came the splintering of wood and the hinges parted company with the lintel. He stumbled to his knees in the wide hallway beyond, hitting the floor so hard with his legs that the blow brought a sudden grunt of agony to his lips.

He didn't know what he would find inside that room. All he knew was that horror had been there and had left its mark. He could smell the stench of evil and corruption in his nostrils and there was the electric tautness in the air that tingled along his nerves, lancing into his brain with a physical agony.

'Paul! Are you all right?' His voice came out in tense gasps. He pushed himself to his feet, stood swaying for a long moment trying to pull himself together.

The silence in the house was complete. The fear was rising in his throat. The muscles of his stomach knotted suddenly and cramped so hard that the pain ran through his entire body.

'Paul!'

The silence continued. He didn't wait for an answer then but did what he had to do. Swiftly, in a couple of loping strides, he reached the closed door leading into the front room. It swung open as he pushed hard against it and he almost fell through into the room beyond.

And then the picture was almost complete. He saw several things in a single glance, but for the first few seconds, they were curiously disconnected.

Paul Chambers lay outstretched on the rug in front of the fire, his arms outflung, his legs twisted oddly beneath his body. Flames were already beginning to lick around the edge of the carpet and yet it was obvious that the fire had not been the cause.

All this he saw instantly, the picture burning itself indelibly on his mind. But it was the thing near the window that caught and held his attention. The fear formed like a whisper inside his mind, rose up swiftly, knotting his muscles, so that he was unable to move.

It had shape, but seemed to be made of shadow stuff, but the eyes that glared at him out of the shadow of the face were red and loathsome, filled with evil and hatred, malevolent and frightening. He almost screamed out aloud with the sudden, shocking realisation. That fiendish thing from the manor on the hill.

He tried to utter a prayer, but the words stuck in his throat and refused to come. He wanted to make the sign of the cross in front of him, to protect him in some manner from this terrible, loathsome creature from the nethermost pit of hell. But the eyes that glared at him seemed to possess some strange quality which slapped his hand down against his side as though by physical force.

He took a gasping, shuddering breath that sent a stab of pain through his lungs. He tried to think, to pull himself together and still the trembling in his limbs. How long he stood there with those frightening eyes boring into his, it was impossible even to estimate. To him it seemed like an eternity.

There were little pricklings in his arms and legs, fire in his body. He wanted to scream but no sound came. His lips were pressed back against his teeth in a snarl of defiance, until they began to hurt. With a tremendous effort, he tore his eyes away from that hypnotic gaze, looked down at his feet. There was nothing he could do, but why hadn't Chambers done something? Chambers who was supposed to know all of the answers.

He grew aware that his eyes were riveted on something small and glittering on the carpet as his feet. Several seconds fled before he realised what it was. The tiny golden crucifix that he had seen Chambers throw at that creature back at the de Ruys manor. If it had worked then, it might work now.

Almost as if it had divined his intentions, the creature near the window suddenly uttered a low, diabolical laugh, a frightening sound that sent shivers along his nerves.

He didn't want to bend and pick it up. He sensed what horror might be let loose. But he knew that he had to, if he wanted to survive. He reached forward. Something evil touched his mind. Panic tore through him. He had to look up into those eyes, he *had* to! But he didn't. Instead, with a sudden lunge, he jerked himself forward.

The lights dimmed. The fire seemed to become dampened down until it gave only a feeble glow; and even that threatened to die out altogether, leaving the room in complete darkness. There was a spine-chilling shriek of laughter from the corner of the room. He saw the figure glide forward, fingers outstretched, reaching for him.

It was getting hard to breathe. The very air seemed thick and viscous, as if he were bending down through molasses. The laughter ripped at his ears. For a moment there was fury. The lights had dimmed so that he could scarcely see. His fingers touched the soft pile of the carpet, fumbled around desperately. *Oh God, where was it?*

His throat constricted. There was a throbbing ache at the back of his temples. He was completely blind. The loathsome thing came closer. Something touched him on the arm. An icy blast swirled about him. There was the sickly stench of decay and corruption in his nostrils, the smell of the grave and things long-dead. He was shivering uncontrollably, his mind reeling.

His fingers touched something cold

and smooth. Instinctively, he clutched it tightly, brought it up, held it out in front of his face. The creature shied away from him as if it had come up against a red-hot wall. The lights in the room flickered and began to brighten slightly. The fire in the hearth burst into life again, burning feebly.

He walked slowly forward, holding the crucifix in front of him at arm's length. Slowly, reluctantly, the creature retreated before him. It reached the wall.

'*In nomine Patris, et Filii, et Spiritus Sancti.*' He spoke the words slowly and clearly, mildly surprised to find that he could speak again.

Hatred glared at him briefly out of the red eyes. He clearly saw the features of the creature for the first time. An insane face, skeletal, the skin lying close to the bone structure, the wispy hair on the balding head glinting white in the returning firelight. For one wild moment, he thought that the crucifix would not be sufficient to protect him. Then a hideous snarl spread over the harsh, cruel features. It was a snarl of thwarted desire and defeat. Almost before Fenner was aware of it, the thing began to fade, slowly, reluctantly, until he could see the details of the wall through it. When it went altogether, he wasn't sure. But suddenly, he knew that it wasn't there any longer and the pressure in his mind was gone.

An overwhelming feeling of exhaustion crept over him. He felt as though something had been drained out of him by the horrible experience just past; something which could never be replaced, *Oh God*, he thought fiercely, *where would this terrible thing end?*

He turned back to Chambers, lying face downward on the rug. The flames were licking around the carpet now, threatening to engulf the whole room, to devour his friend's body before he could prevent it. Swiftly, he stamped at them until they were extinguished. The edges of the carpet had been badly burned, but that was all.

Swiftly, he went down on one knee, rolled the other over, felt for the pulse. At first, he could detect nothing and a sudden fit of panic seized him. It was difficult to keep his fingers from trembling again and he lifted his head, and forced himself to stare fixedly at the opposite wall and put everything out of his mind, while he concentrated every sense on feeling for the pulse. Finally, he detected it, swift and irregular. He loosened the other's collar and placed one of the cushions under his head.

Chambers stirred feebly. His eyes were half-open, but the muscles of his face were stiff and rigid, lumped under the skin. The collar of his shirt was limp and soaked with sweat. He tried to push himself up on to his elbow and by now, his eyes were wide open, staring fixedly at Fenner, his left hand stretched out in front of him, fingers clenched as though trying to ward something off, something terrible.

'Steady now. Paul. For God's sake take it easy. You're all right now.'

'*Oh, God!*'

'I know,' said Fenner gently. He slipped his hands under the other's armpits and held him up, easing him across to the chair where Chambers sank back, eyes still staring, but a little of the fear beginning to go out of them.

'What can you possibly know, John?' The other's voice was little more than a dry, husky whisper.

Fenner shivered. 'Enough to guess at what happened. That thing was still here when I burst into the room.'

'I thought so. It came here to destroy me. I tried to stop it but I failed.' His voice started to shake and he clasped his hands in front of his face as though to shut out the scene.

Fenner said thickly; 'Just sit back and relax. I'll get a drink for you. It will steady your nerves.'

He poured the drink for the other, then got one for himself. Gulping it down, he felt a little better.

Chambers laid an unsteady hand on Fenner's arm. 'How did you manage to defeat it?'

'With the crucifix. It was lying on the carpet, I guessed you must have tried to use it, but without success. I wasn't sure that it would be enough to scare it off. I

91

remembered that you said some time ago that these inhuman creatures would get stronger and more dangerous.'

'I know.' The other sipped his brandy slowly. A little of the colour was coming back into his face. 'I was a fool, I suppose. But never for a single moment did I think it would dare to venture abroad like that, even at night. It must have been terrible for you, not being prepared for anything like that. You can thank your lucky stars that you had the presence of mind to use the crucifix. It was the only thing, in the circumstances, which could have saved you.'

A log fell, spitting and spluttering, into the hearth. Fenner felt his heart leap at the sudden, unexpected sound. 'Is this thing all-powerful then except when we can use the crucifix against it?'

'No, not exactly. The Undead are powerful, that's true, but they do have certain limitations. Their power is at its lowest, although not lost altogether, during the hours of daylight. Except at sunset and sunrise, they cannot cross running water, no matter what form they take. Nor can they eat human food. As you know, the cross is anathema as far as they are concerned while both garlic and honeysuckle are potent things which can be used against them.'

'Do you think it will come back tonight?'

'I only wish to God I knew. They don't usually give up as easily as that . . . I'm thinking it must have had some reason for wanting to kill me. Probably I know too much.'

Fenner sat down in the chair opposite Chambers. He was sweating and his hands were shaking.

The Undead.

It struck him then how appropriate the words were to describe these inhuman creatures. Somewhere, lost inside him, a tiny voice was shrieking: *They'll come back, all five of them and the next time, there'll be no escape.*

'What do you think we ought to do, Paul?' he asked finally, when he could trust himself to speak evenly. 'Those creatures up on the hill have got to be destroyed.'

'That's far easier said than done, John. 'We can't take the chance of going up there by ourselves, especially after sunset.'

No, Fenner thought, that would be asking for trouble. Insanity, perhaps, as the brain snapped at the horror of what it saw. Like Pendrake's wife who had talked of terrible things before she had finally died, completely insane. He recalled the look on Pendrake's face when he had last seen him and shivered.

'But we've got to go up there, Paul. And tonight. We've no other alternative. God knows what diabolical horror they intend to perpetrate next.'

'We can't, John. We've nothing to protect us.'

'The crucifix worked before — '

'In daylight. Their power is weakened then. Now, it will be vastly different.'

'Then I will have to go alone,' Fenner said tightly, 'if you refuse to come with me. I'll take my revolver. If these things can be killed by physical means, then rest assured they will be.'

'No, John. That is a fool's way. Are you

so tired of living that you want to throw your life away?'

Fenner shook his head sadly. 'I don't *want* to do anything of the kind. But it's now or never. If we don't make an attempt to destroy these loathsome things, they could bring untold horror to the village. It's now or not at all. The longer we wait the more dangerous it will be.'

The other was obviously still filled with the horrible fear of his recent experience. He poured himself another stiff glass of brandy and downed it at a single gulp, in an effort to steady his frayed nerves.

'Well, maybe the odds aren't so heavily weighed against us,' he muttered, getting to his feet and warming his hands at the fire. 'We might stand a chance — '

The sharp ringing of the telephone interrupted his words. He crossed over to the phone, lifted the receiver from its cradle and spoke rapidly:

'Hello. Chambers here.'

Fenner heard the thin-sounding voice at the other end of the wire, but could not distinguish the words. Then abruptly, there seemed to be a slight change in the tone of the other's voice. It rose in pitch, then became choked off quite suddenly, as if a hand had been clamped around the speaker's throat.

A look of abrupt horror spread rapidly over Chambers' features as he slammed down the phone. He stared across at Fenner and said tightly:

'That was Kennaway. He said there was something trying to get in, to get at him. Then there was that horrible choking cough. Oh my God, what is loose in the village now?'

Fenner was on his feet in an instant, the brandy in his glass forgotten. 'The only thing we can do now is to find out. Bring whatever you think we need to protect us from these evil things.'

'Of course,' stammered the other. He seemed to shake himself mentally.

'We'll stop off at my place and collect the gun. Even though it may not help us, I'd feel safer with it.'

Ten minutes later, straining their eyes and ears for every sound and movement from the dark shadows of the trees lining the narrow lane leading to the house where Kennaway lived, they made their way slowly forward.

The house came in sight.

Behind the curtains, all was in utter darkness. There wasn't a single sound to disturb the clinging pall of silence that hung over the place.

They entered the gate and walked very slowly along the gravel drive. In the faint starlight, they could make out the front porch, gleaming faintly in the dim light. Tall lilac bushes dotted the wide expanse of lawn in front of the building. A twisted yew stood isolated at one corner of the house, branches rising up against the sky like clutching fingers, clawing at the clouds and the stars, seeking to pull them down from heaven.

Chambers hesitated.

'What's wrong?' murmured Fenner tautly. His fingers closed over the butt of the revolver in his pocket and there was a cool reassurance in the solid feel of the heavy metal.

'There's something nearby, I can feel it. But I can't see it.'

'Probably it's still inside the house with Kennaway, and good God, his wife will be there too. What in heaven's name can have happened to her?'

'I don't know, but we mustn't go rushing in there with our eyes shut, trusting to blind luck to protect us. At least, we can prepare ourselves with what few things we have.'

He pulled something out of his pocket, something that glittered in the starlight. Fenner, glancing down, saw that it was a small glass phial of some kind filled with a colourless liquid. He regarded it curiously, trying to fight down the natural urgency in his mind. He tried to tell himself that what the other had said, what he was doing, was the only sensible thing in the circumstances. They could save no one if they went in there, unprotected, and were destroyed themselves in the process.

'First,' whispered Chambers, 'we must seal every entrance of our body with this holy water. Fortunately, I brought some back with me from Lourdes three years ago. It's extremely potent against all forms of evil. At least it will give us a first line of defence if nothing else.'

Fenner waited impatiently and a little sceptically, while the other made the sign of the cross in holy water over his eyes ears and nose. Then he did the same for the other. All the time, the house, fifty feet away, stood in darkness in a brooding silence. Even at that distance, it was possible to see that the curtains over one of the lower windows had been thrown aside, as though twitched across the window by someone peering out into the dimness.

'Now, we're almost ready,' whispered Chambers. He held out the tiny plaited wreath of garlic flowers to the other: 'Keep these in a safe place, particularly where they're exposed. If only we had a little of the Sacred Host, it would be possible for us to walk unharmed through the nethermost regions of Hell itself. But that is something you cannot get without a special dispensation.'

Carefully, they moved along the gravel path. Although Fenner knew these grounds well, having visited Kennaway and his attractive wife many times in the past the moonlit darkness seemed to alter everything, to give even the most innocuous details a nightmarish appearance.

'I don't like this silence at all,' murmured Chambers, pausing beside one of the lilac bushes. 'It could mean that the creature has already destroyed them or is still there, lying in wait for us.'

'Could Kennaway somehow have managed to scare it off as I did?'

'I doubt that. If he had, the lights would all have been on. They don't like the light in any shape or form.'

Chambers eased his way forward until he reached the side of the porch. Fenner joined him, eased the gun out of his pocket, checked it automatically, then took off the safety catch. No telling when they would need it, nor how quickly. Better not to take chances.

Chambers walked across the creaking boards of the porch, reached the door and tried it gently. It swung open at his touch. Beyond, was darkness.

As Fenner came up to him, Chambers stepped inside, fumbled along the wall, feeling for the light switch. It snapped down with a sudden explosive click.

The lights came on, shone brilliantly in the room. Fenner peered over the other's shoulder, could see nothing out of the ordinary.

'Kennaway! Where the devil are you?'

No answer. The silence was everywhere in that house like a tangible thing, squeezing itself out of the walls around them.

'Kennaway. For God's sake answer, man!'

Chambers stared wildly around the room, his mouth working horribly as he tried to control his nerves. Swiftly Fenner walked to the door on the far side of the room, jerked it open. It was a cupboard. Clothing hung on pegs along the back, but it was otherwise empty. He closed the door, the feeling of impending disaster growing strong within him. A sense of evil seemed to hang in the air.

He opened the other door, found himself in the kitchen. Everything was in place. Chambers was already leaping for the stairs, shouting Kennaway's name at the top of the stairs. Fenner followed close on the other's heels. At the top, there was a short corridor.

Chambers jerked open one of the doors, peered inside after switching on the light, gave a muffled curse, slammed the door and pointed to the second door a few yards further along the corridor.

'In there,' he gasped. 'See if there's anyone there. They must be around here somewhere.'

Fenner reached the other door in a couple of strides, thrust it open. The room was in darkness and there was the most curious sensation in his mind as he fumbled for the light switch.

Chambers thrust against him from behind, peering tensely over his shoulder.

'My God! It's Mrs. Kennaway!'

Fenner went down on one knee and gently turned her over. The look of horror and revulsion on her face made him feel physically and mentally sick.

'Is she — ?'

Fenner got swiftly to his feet, crossed over to the dressing table and picked up the small crystal mirror. Going back, he placed it in front of the woman's lips, held it there for a few moments. Not a single trace of moisture misted the clear surface of the glass.

'She's dead, I'm afraid, Paul. There's nothing I can do for her now.'

'Oh, my God. But what on earth could have killed her? There doesn't seem to be any mark of violence on her body.'

'From the expression on her face I'd say off-hand that she died of fright. Fear can be a potent thing, Paul.'

'Was her heart in a weak state at all?'

'Not that I know of. I examined her several times and her heart was as strong as yours or mine. But if she saw anything like that which I saw in your room tonight, then I'm not surprised that she had heart failure.'

'But where's Kennaway himself?' the other gasped out. He looked about him wildly. 'He isn't here.'

'Can those creatures have got him?' A confusion of riotous ideas possessed Fenner's brain. His eyes seemed unable to tear themselves away from the twisted, distorted face of the once beautiful woman at his feet. Now it was a thing of frightful distortion, the eyes wide and staring, looking past him, fixedly having seen something that it was not good for human eyes to see. Oh God, he thought frenziedly, no wonder Pendrake's wife had gone insane, living with that half-crazy old man in that accursed house up there on the top of the hill. The wonder was that she had lived so long in the midst of all that horror. He turned slowly and looked at his companion.

'There's nothing more we can do here. Paul,' he said harshly. 'I suggest that we go through with our original plan. This makes it only more urgent. We've got to destroy her killer before it strikes anywhere else; and above all, we must find Kennaway.'

'We'll never find him now,' said the other dully. 'He'll be tucked away somewhere where we can never find him. If he's still alive, then God have mercy on his soul. If he's dead, really dead, then perhaps that's all for the best.'

'I'm still going up there,' muttered Fenner stubbornly. 'If you'll come with me, then I'll feel a little safer. But if you won't come, and after seeing this I can't really blame you, then I must go and try and find Kennaway myself. The evil up there in that house cannot be allowed to go unchecked.'

'Very well.' The other sighed, threw a final glance at the woman on the floor, then followed Fenner out of the room. In the corridor, he said thinly. 'What are you going to do about Mrs. Kennaway?'

'When we get back, I'll inform the coroner, of course. It won't be difficult to establish the reason for her death, although the cause might be a little more obscure.'

'*If* we get back,' corrected the other hoarsely.

They made their way outside, across the lawn, into the trees at the end of the gravel drive. Patches of yellow moonlight picked out the bushes that bordered the lawn etching the drive with shadow. Fenner shivered. Somewhere out there, God alone knew where, was Kennaway.

They turned into the lane. It stretched away in front of them like a river of midnight, dark and forbidding. There was the musty smell of rotting wood, or dead leaves underfoot — and something else which assailed his nostrils, faint and far away. He had smelt it several times before. Once up at the de Ruys manor when they had seen that abomination in the doorway, in Chambers's room, and faintly in the house they had just left.

He shivered. Why had Kennaway been taken away and the body of his wife left behind? It didn't make sense, but he had the idea that they would find the answer to it up there on top of the hill, probably in that deserted, mouldering graveyard, that patch of unhallowed ground at the back of the manor.

Very soon, they were out of the village and toiling along the half-obliterated road that led up to the hilltop.

In the darkness, they were glad of the moonlight though it made the shadowed ground far more ominous than complete darkness itself. Things seemed to move on the edge of their vision; terrible, grotesque things that vanished, or crouched still and immobile whenever they turned their heads to look directly at them.

More candles would have to be lit in the village, more prayers mumbled, if they did not succeed in what they had to do. They topped a low rise. The moonlight flooded all about them, lighting everything.

Chambers stumbled forward beside him, his breath coming in harsh gasps. His face seemed ashen and bloodless in the moonlight and every few moments, he would pause and lift his head, staring directly ahead of him, as though anticipating the horror that inevitably lay in front of them. Over everything loomed the vast, black shadow of the manor, dark against the moonlit sky.

Then something moved, two or three hundred yards in front of them, moving from boulder to boulder where the roadway had been obliterated altogether. For a moment, he could scarcely believe his eyes.

That terrible, loathsome, loping thing which bounded from concealing shadow to concealing shadow and that other shape which it carried, the shape which was oddly human and which he knew, instinctively, was Kennaway.

5

Sussamma Ritual

Paul Chambers saw the creature in the same instant, clutched at the other's arm as he almost fell. Here was the red madness of diabolism. The night suddenly grew hideous with things that were beyond all human comprehension and imagination. There was nothing in Fenner's mind to allow him to describe that evil entity which moved steadily upward, over the rough ground, towards the dark manor high above.

Here, he knew, was some blasphemous abnormality from the nethermost reaches of hell itself. Something which had died over three centuries before, but which had lived in some hideous way, sustaining its existence on Earth by some unearthly means at which he could only guess. Possibly Pendrake had known of its existence and it was a certainty that his wife had. Mrs. Kennaway must have seen it in all its gruesome horror in that split second before the shock had proved too much for her and she had died back there in that silent, evil-tainted house.

The shadow was still just visible as it moved up through vague patches of moonlight. Whether or not it was human, whether or not it was the same thing with the red eyes which Fenner had encountered less than a couple of hours earlier in Chambers's room, it was impossible to tell. The old tales spoke of five of the de Ruys family who were buried in that unhallowed ground. If one managed to come back, if the evil was crystallised there for one of them, might it not be the same for the others? The thought almost broke him in half.

He pulled himself sharply together, caught hold of the other by the elbow and urged him forward. 'Now's the time to use some of the White Magic you claim to know, Paul,' he hissed sharply.

'It may not be enough,' murmured the other fearfully. 'We're up against something far stronger than anything I've ever known in all of my life. This is something from the pit of hell itself.'

'We must go on. We can't afford to turn back now,' insisted Fenner harshly. He thrust himself forward over the slippery rocks, half-dragging the other with him. A gust of cold air swirled about them as they moved slowly upward. He lifted his head and tried to spot the abominable creature again, but it seemed to have vanished into the general darkness which lay at the base of the house, and which seemed to be clustered far more intensely there than anywhere else on the entire side of the hill.

Time ceased to exist for either of them as they toiled their way up the steep slope. To Fenner, it seemed as if they were forcing their way forward against something invisible that resisted their movements. As they neared the top of the hill an unearthly chill seemed to creep down from the black-shadowed manor, swirling and eddying about them as a cold river current suddenly strikes a man swimming in the water.

'Keep moving,' muttered Fenner

harshly as he thrust his way forward.

An utter silence filled the air in front of them. The grotesque shadow with its human burden had disappeared into the manor — or had it moved around the side of it to that dreadful place at the back?

Finally they reached the top and stood gasping with the exertion, breathing heavily, their hearts thudding against their ribs.

Fenner stared about him, feeling the coldness in his body growing stronger with every passing second. Even though the workmen had done their work well, and it was scarcely recognisable in many places, there was still that air of evil hanging over the house. That, he knew, was something that would always be there no matter what Angela de Ruys tried to do to get rid of it. You couldn't wipe out the evil of three hundred years in a few weeks.

In the darkness, where the moonlight failed to penetrate, there was nothing that they could see. Nothing moved and there was no sound.

Beside him, as they walked forward

into the half-finished house, Chambers began to intone a prayer, speaking softly and continuously, not raising his voice above the murmur of the wind which had suddenly and inexplicably sprung up around them. And yet, in spite of the softness of the words, they seemed to ring out clearly and forcefully.

Inside the house, where part of the roof lay open to the sky, their footsteps echoed hollowly. Fenner fancied that he saw vague shapes and shadows moving at the top of the winding stairway, but he couldn't be sure and his fingers tightened convulsively around the butt of the revolver as he pulled it from his pocket and held it in his right hand. A faint, low moaning sound became perceptible as they walked slowly through the house. It seemed to originate from somewhere at the top of the stairs, but Fenner couldn't be sure and Chambers walked with his head down, looking intently at the ground under his feet, almost as if he were afraid to lift his head in case he saw something fronting him.

After a few moments, Fenner began to

feel a return of a little of his confidence. No ghostly shape had risen up in front of them to bar their way. There were no sounds in the house apart from the low moaning which was probably nothing more than the wind sighing through the half-open windows upstairs. But then, as the seconds passed, they seemed to be faced with a new and unaccountable phenomenon. There seemed to be a faint glow in the darkness all around them. It wasn't the moonlight. Rather it seemed a ghastly glow, reminiscent of a fire seen from a distance reflected from the undersides of lowering, threatening thunderclouds. Within moments, he knew that it was not merely a product of his imagination. There was scarcely any feeling in his legs and arms as the terrible cold ate into his limbs. His fingers around the trigger of the gun felt stiff and inflexible. The glow seemed to flicker insidiously under the increasing strength of the icy blast of air that swept around them.

A wave of sickness surged up from the pit of his stomach. The dull monotonous intoning of the other's voice began to get on his nerves. He wanted to shriek out aloud, to tell him to stop. Then came the realisation that this was probably just what the Enemy wanted. There was some subtle probing into his mind. They were getting at him, not at Chambers.

There was a sudden diabolical chuckle from the shadows at the corner of the room. Some horror was forming inside the ring of shadow.

Two points of red satanic light appeared on a level with their eyes. Then the thing gradually took shape. A long, dark, almost beast-like face, that leered at them from the dimness.

Chambers was mouthing words automatically now, cold perspiration breaking out on his face. Fenner's nails bit deeply into the palm of his left hand as he watched the shape move forward, slowly, the features alive with a terrible, demoniacal light.

'Oh God,' he gasped thickly. 'What the devil is it?'

Chambers continued to pray loudly, raising his voice this time as much as he could. But even then the words were almost completely drowned out by the fiendish chuckling and the moaning from above their heads that now seemed to rise to a shrieking crescendo.

'Whatever it is, don't look at its eyes.' The other's words probed through the mental fog that threatened to engulf Fenner's brain. 'Don't look at the eyes!'

Desperately, he tried to drag his gaze away from those terrible points of light, but found it impossible to do so, Instinctively, some part of his brain detached but oddly alert, told him that Chambers was staring directly at the floor under his feet, not once looking up as he went back to praying.

The creature's eyes seemed to expand to grow into pools of liquid fire. Almost of their own volition, his feet took one shuffling step forward. He knew what he was doing, knew that it was madness to walk forward like that, but there was nothing he could do to help himself. Chambers had a tight grip on his arm, but he tried desperately to shake it off. There was a voice in the room other than his companion's, muttering the most terrible obscenities and seconds fled, before he realised that it was his own.

The thing was only two yards away from him now, the face leering into his, mocking him silently, as if daring him to try to tear his gaze away. He knew with a shudder of fear that it was utterly beyond his strength to do so. He tried madly to press the trigger of the gun in his right hand. But the numbness there seemed complete. His finger refused to obey his faltering will. His feet took another step forward, his shoe rasping over the rough, wooden floor. There was another fearsome laugh of positive devilish glee.

With one swift movement, Chambers had another tight grip on his left arm, hauling him back with all of his strength.

'Try to look away, John. God help us now, God help us.'

At that positive suggestion, the thing stepped back a couple of paces. It seemed to shrink in upon itself a little, to quiver slightly as though struck by something invisible.

Then it came forward again, but this

time, the chuckle was one of thwarted desire and malice.

Through all that timeless interval which may have been seconds or days, Fenner fought to look away from those terrible eyes. His entire being seemed to be swamped and enveloped by those twin pools of redness. Then, when it seemed that he must be drowned in them forever, he felt, rather than saw, Chambers lift something in his right hand, at the same time, uttering something in a language that he didn't recognise. The effect was instantaneous. The creature seemed to shrink away into the wall. The red eyes dimmed and he suddenly found that he had use of his limbs once more.

Instinctively, his finger tightened on the trigger of the revolver and he fired it three times in rapid succession. The flashing glare of the shots lit up the room as though by lightning flashes. He could even see the details of the far wall through the fading body of the loathsome thing. A piercing scream, harsh and shrill with anger and baffled pain, rang through the room. The red glow from the wall faded to a faint rosy hue, then went out altogether and they were left in the clinging darkness.

Fenner's hands were shaking violently as he lowered the gun, stood staring for a moment into the darkness, scarcely comprehending the stupendous fact that the inhuman fiend had gone, then turned slowly to face the other.

'One of those creatures without a doubt,' said Chambers as the other described, haltingly, what he had seen. 'But where are the others? And where is Kennaway? They've taken him for some purpose. We must find him.'

Now it was Chambers who seemed determined to go through with the task they had set themselves. He walked swiftly through the room, pausing only as they entered one at the rear of the house, overlooking the five graves that lay silent in the yellow moonlight. For the first time, since they had entered the house, Chambers used the torch he had brought along with him. He shone it on to the floor in front of them. There was a faded carpet there that had obviously been laid there by Pendrake. One glance around the room was sufficient to show them that the workmen repairing the place had not yet come to this wing of the house.

Chambers went forward swiftly, plucked savagely at the edge of the carpet and pulled it aside with a swift movement. Dust rose in a grey cloud into the air. The beam of the torch flicked over the dusty floor underneath.

At first, Fenner could see nothing out of the ordinary. Then, under the thick layer of dust, it was possible for him to make out the tracery of the design that had been daubed on the wooden floor. The five-pointed pentacle could just be discerned, surrounded by a broad white circle. With his shoe, Chambers scraped away some of the dust, revealing the strange, half-frightening cabalistic figures around the circumference more clearly.

'Everything that I had suspected. We ought to have looked for this earlier. Even though we could not have gone to the police with such a wild story, this would have been sufficient to verify our fears and there are still people, even today, who would have listened and helped us.'

'But Kennaway. Surely he hasn't been brought here for this. What do you say it is — the Black Mass?'

'I doubt it. All this was daubed on the floor a long time ago. This must have been the room where those fiendish creatures in the seventeenth century practised their evil rites until their dark master tired of them and either drove them insane or killed them. This would explain everything. Where they gained the power to continue their evil.'

'And you believe that Pendrake knew of this too?'

'He must have done. Heaven help us, this is even worse than I had feared.' Chambers let the carpet fall back into place.

They went out through the open door at the back of the house, into the moonlight and the shadow of the manor. The headstones glistened faintly in the moonlight as though covered with moisture and dripping fungoid growths of hideous shape. Fenner blinked and tried to see beyond them. An empty stretch of ground which reached back for close on fifty yards before it tumbled down the rear slope of the hill, towards the heath which lay down below, stretching away to Kenton a few miles distant. The moon slipped behind a ragged cloud. In the darkness every little shape seemed to have been magnified a hundred-fold, exaggerated out of all proportion.

But before the moon had vanished, he had seen the dark shape that lay slumped between the headstones face downwards on the foetid earth.

Kennaway!

He started forward. A quick grab at the other's inert form and maybe they could drag him away from this terrible place before there was any further manifestation of evil.

He had advanced two steps when he suddenly caught the feel of eyes watching him. Go forward to Kennaway and they would be out in the open. Death would be waiting for them there.

Chambers too had seen the body of their friend. He stood irresolute for a moment, obviously aware of the same thing. Then the moon came out and they saw the five dark figures standing in the shadow of the tall yews. Evil emanated from them so strongly that Fenner could feel it swirling around him in titanic waves. Three men and two women, dressed as he would have guessed they would have been attired in life, but the mould of the grave was on them and there was nothing lifelike about them.

Remembering the other's earlier warning, Fenner forced himself not to look at their eyes, but lifted his gaze and stared at the branches of the trees behind them, outlined starkly against the sky.

The leafless branches were twitching, even though the wind had died away completely and even the grass was rustling on the ground.

If Chambers had noticed this weird phenomenon he gave no outward sign. Out of the corner of his vision Fenner saw the other try to lift his hand to make the sign of the cross in front of them, but it seemed to be slapped instantly down against his side as the baleful glare from the redly-glowing eyes fell upon him. It was as if there was a physical force, unheard and invisible, around them.

A dark cloud passed over the face of the moon. Everything was eclipsed in the darkness that followed. The shaking silhouette of the spasmodically jerking branches faded abruptly and when the moon came out again, flooding the scene with light, everything was normal, except for the five figures which had moved out into the open, standing among the headstones, less than two feet from the inert body which lay between them.

The two men paused indecisively as the aura of evil grew stronger.

Savagely, Fenner tried to hold on to his buckling consciousness. He felt a sudden clutching at his heart as though an icy hand had curled about it and was squeezing the life out of him inexorably.

He glanced wildly about him, seeking some way of escape. But something seemed to hold him rooted to the spot, unable to move a single muscle. He could see that the earth over the five graves had a fresh look about it, as though it had been newly dug or burst open from underneath.

The foul, leprous things glided forward, noiselessly, with an unearthly motion.

How long they stood there, tensed with horror, facing those awful shadows, Fenner never knew, yet he became suddenly aware that they were close to him, less than three feet away. There was a strange kind of substance about them, a shimmering reality, as though they were standing in some form of heat haze that made their outline vague and indistinct. The very smell of evil was in the air, the sweet and cloying charnel stench of the rotting grave.

There was that laughter again, ringing in their ears, mocking them both with the diabolical knowledge that it possessed the power to destroy them both in spite of what they could do against the evil that was here. Waves of satanic power rippled towards them, threatening to engulf them utterly.

Nothing could possibly stop these creatures now that their evil power was at its height. They were indestructible so long as the darkness was there all around them and only the moon shone on the scene.

They drew their life from the darkness of the night and even the garlic seemed to have no effect on them; nor the golden crucifix that Chambers had taken from his pocket and was striving desperately to lift in front of his face, with arms that seemed suddenly devoid of any strength.

His mouth was working horribly as he stood there, leaning forward slightly, as though held up by something invisible.

Then, sharply and in a clear, ringing voice, Chambers spoke something in an unknown language that Fenner could not understand. The effect was immediate. The moonlight seemed to brighten perceptibly. Something bright that hurt their eyes swirled about the evil creatures that stood in front of them. Fenner had the impression that it snatched at them like a sheet of flame. There was a rushing sound in his ears like a distant peal of thunder, then silence.

With an effort, he opened his eyes and looked about him. Gradually, as his eyes became more accustomed to the moon-light, he saw the inert figure of Kennaway lying where he had been before, among the headstones. Of the five creatures that had been there a few moments earlier, there was no sign. The wind that blew on his face was cold, but fresh, clearing his tired, confused brain slowly.

Chambers was breathing heavily beside him. His face was bloodless, his lips trembling slightly.

'What happened?' asked Fenner harshly.

'They're gone. For the moment, anyway. But they haven't been destroyed. The words of the Sussamma Ritual were my last resort, and may only be used to save any souls that are in imminent danger of being destroyed. But quickly — we must get Kennaway out of here while we have the chance.'

Fenner hurried forward and bent beside the body on the ground, felt for the pulse. For a moment, he could detect nothing, then, feeble and faint, he felt it, and breathed a sigh of relief. Although still alive, there was no way of telling what his mental condition would be like once the full horror of the situation made itself known to him.

Together, they managed to lift him and

carry him around the side of the house, across the lawn, down the wide drive, out through the tall gates with their stone pillars topped by graven wide-winged daemons. Several times, they were forced to halt on the way down the hillside, but finally, exhausted, they reached the bottom and entered the sleeping village.

'We'd better take him to my place,' suggested Chambers after a moment. 'We can't take the risk of taking him back to his own house, not with his wife there. Besides, they may return for him, and if he's with me, I may be able to do something to prevent it.'

Between them, they carried the unconscious form of Kennaway into the other's house and laid him on the bed in the spare room.

'We'll need to watch him closely once he regains consciousness,' said Fenner seriously. 'There's no telling how strong their hold over him may be, nor what he'll try to do once he learns, or even suspects, the truth.'

'If you'd care to stay too for the night, I can put you up,' Chambers suggested.

Fenner nodded his acceptance. 'They say there's safety in numbers,' he said with a wry grin. 'If you're sure it won't be putting you out.'

'It won't,' declared the other firmly. 'I'm quite sure that there'll be no sleep for me tonight.'

'Nor me,' agreed Fenner.

'All right,' said Chambers. 'In the morning, I think we ought to go and have another talk with Miss de Ruys. After what has happened tonight, it would be dangerous folly for her to continue with her plan. We've got to make her see what terrible evil she's unleashing on the village.' He poured himself a stiff brandy, handing one to Fenner.

Gulping it down, Chambers went on: 'Already, that prophecy of Henry de Ruys', is coming into effect. She's got to be made to see that she is the primary cause of it all.'

Fenner remained silent, sipping his drink.

'You don't think she'll change her mind?' queried Chambers. He looked at him closely.

'I'm quite sure she won't. Until she sees what we have seen, she'll never believe it.'

'I see,' muttered the other gravely. 'Then somehow we've just got to persuade her.'

Fenner suddenly remembered Kennaway lying in the other room, unconscious on the bed, unknowing of the full extent of the horror that had befallen him. The thought prompted another in his mind. He walked over to the telephone and called the police.

'Sergeant Weldon?' He licked his lips, then went on: 'Sorry to disturb you at this unearthly hour of the morning, Sergeant. This is Doctor Fenner. I want to report the death of Mrs. Kennaway.'

6

Possession!

' . . . and those are the facts of the matter, Weldon,' Fenner concluded his report to the Police-Sergeant. They were standing outside Kennaway's house.

'You think it could have been anything to do with these rumours that have been flying around the village ever since Pendrake met his death up there in the old house, Doctor?' The Sergeant looked up at him closely through narrowed eyes.

Fenner noticed instantly that the other had used the words 'met his death' rather than merely saying that Pendrake had died. That, in itself, suggested that he was uncertain as to the real cause of the man's death, and had his own suspicions of what might have happened.

'You know what I'm getting at, Doctor,' went on Weldon, peering back at the curtained windows of the silent house.

'Things have been happening here ever since Pendrake died, possibly even before that, if we count the strange affair of his wife. Now this woman has come from America. She says that she's a direct descendant of the family who used to live in the manor. Whether she is or not, is no immediate concern of mine.

'But I do know this. Ever since she's been here things have been happening in the village and rumours have been flying around, which I can't say I like.'

'Do you believe them, Sergeant?'

'I'm not sure, sir. I'd like to say that I don't. I'm not a superstitious man myself, like most of the villagers are — even though I've lived here all of my life. But even though, in my job, you have to be practical about these things, still you have to admit there must be something in them. No matter who you speak to, they all tell you virtually the same thing.'

Something flared briefly in his dark eyes and he licked his lips a trifle apprehensively as he lifted his head and stared moodily at the dark shadow of the manor that lay sprawled over the top of the hill in the distance.

'You know, Doctor, I'm sure there's something going on in that place, especially after dark. Even these workmen won't stay there after the sun's gone down. And I know for a fact that nothing will induce them to stay once it's dark.'

'You heard about Kennaway too, I suppose,' Fenner said.

The other nodded his head sombrely. 'A great pity that. But I suppose it was bound to happen.' He paused, looked up quickly as another thought struck him. 'Say, doctor, you don't think he could have done it, do you? I mean, he might have killed his wife somehow, and then, unable to face up to the truth, he went insane. It would fit the facts as we know them, wouldn't it?'

'The facts as you know them, perhaps. But not as I know them,' Fenner said carefully. He wasn't sure at the moment, just how much of this fiendish affair he could tell the other. It was all right going to the police, even a man like Sergeant Weldon who had lived there all of his life, and tell them that he had seen devil's work up at the de Ruys manor. The logical thing for them to think would be that he too was insane and ought to be locked up.

'That doesn't make much sense to you, Sergeant. I suppose,' he went on slowly. 'I can't prove much of what has really happened, although I know that Mr. Chambers will back up what I say.'

'Go on, Doctor.' The other was completely the professional policeman.

'You're right when you say that there's something happening at the manor up there. What it is, I don't know myself at the moment. All I do know is that it's something not of this world, something we can't explain scientifically. That's why it doesn't come into my province or yours at the moment, because we deal only with practical things that would stand up in a court of law.'

'Murder is a practical thing doctor,' said the other gravely, 'and if you've any reason to believe that Mrs. Kennaway's death wasn't an accident or from natural causes, then it does come into my province.'

'I realise that, Sergeant. I know her heart was as sound as yours or mine; and from the look on her face, I'd say she died of fright. What happened to her husband is even more difficult to explain and almost impossible to believe.'

'Suppose you tell me it all in your own words, Doctor and let me be the judge,' suggested the other. There was a little snap to his voice. Fenner remembered that he had been a good friend of the Kennaways and he knew that once Weldon got it into his head that Mrs. Kennaway's death was neither accident nor caused by natural events, he wouldn't let go of the case until he had got to the bottom of it.

Fenner explained briefly to the other what had happened during the previous night and early morning. When he had finished, he waited for the other to speak. For a moment, there was silence.

Weldon looked at him curiously, then turned his head and peered up at the manor, looming darkly in the crisp morning air. A few of the workmen were just visible around it even from that distance. 'You say that Paul Chambers saw these creatures too?'

'He was with me all the time. We both went up to that place when we found that Kennaway had gone.'

Weldon looked down at the ground under his feet, frowning. 'If anyone else had told me that story, Doctor, I'd have had them certified as a raving lunatic. I'd have said that they had gone the same way as Mrs. Pendrake or Mr. Kennaway. But I've known you for three years and Paul Chambers almost ten.' He paused, then went on sharply, 'But damn it all, Doctor. These things don't happen these days. They're old wives' tales.'

'That's what I keep trying to tell myself. But three people have died and one man is hopelessly insane. You can't shrug that off as imagination.'

'I see.' The other bit his lip indecisively. In the house, there was a sudden movement and a moment later, two men came out carrying the body of Mrs. Kennaway on a stretcher, a sheet over her face. John Fenner watched the stretcher being carried along the winding path to

135

the waiting van. A few moments later, it drove off and everything was silent again.

'I think we'd better go back, Doctor,' said the other. 'There's nothing more we can do here. What do you intend to put on the certificate?'

'Heart failure. There's nothing else I can do. I wouldn't keep my job long if I said it was due to supernatural causes, would I?'

They walked back in silence to the police station.

'I'll have a couple of men search that house from top to bottom,' said Weldon as he closed the door behind them. 'Though I doubt whether they'll find anything there. Do you think that Kennaway himself will ever be able to tell us what happened there last night?'

'I'm not sure. In his present condition, I doubt it very much. But he may improve. Particularly if we can get him away from these surroundings. They may also be able to use shock therapy on him, although the shock of what he saw and experienced may have been far too great, even for that to succeed. I'll let you know, of course, if he ever does recover sufficiently to be questioned. But it won't be for some time yet.'

'Just one more thing, Doctor. When you intend to go on another of these nocturnal ventures, I'd be glad if you'd let me know. The next time, I'd like to be there, just to satisfy my own curiosity.'

Fenner nodded. 'I'll do that, Sergeant,' he said tightly.

Outside, in the clear morning air, he stood hesitantly on the pavement for a moment, collecting his scattered thoughts. His brain still felt muzzy and confused. He wondered how Chambers was feeling. Then he remembered that he had to see Angela de Ruys, to try to stop her from continuing this idea of hers to stay in that place.

He started to walk towards the Inn, then changed his mind and turned into the narrow street towards Chambers's house. It might add more force to his arguments if he took the other along with him. She might not believe his own unsupported word. And there was something more to it than that. He had the feeling that she thought he was trying to dissuade her from going ahead with her plans for some reason of his own.

⋆ ⋆ ⋆

Angela de Ruys opened the door and eyed them with a trace of hostility. No doubt about it, thought Fenner grimly, she doesn't seem very pleased to see us.

She forced a quick laugh. 'Why, Doctor Fenner and Mr. Chambers. I presume this is something more than a social call, even at this time of the morning.'

Fenner nodded and went inside, followed by Chambers. 'We'd like to have a talk with you, Miss de Ruys,' he began quietly. He lowered himself into one of the chairs. The girl remained standing.

'A talk?' Her voice was like ice, 'I don't think we have anything to talk about. Doctor.'

'I'm quite sure we have,' said Chambers, interrupting. 'You see, since we last met, several things have happened, all of which are connected, indirectly with you.'

'With me?' For a second, as the girl sat

down in the other chair, Fenner could have sworn that he saw a swift look of fear flicker in her eyes. 'I don't understand. What could possibly concern me?'

'Do you know anything of what happened last night?' asked Fenner tightly.

The girl's face hardened, then she said thinly: 'If you mean about your friend Kennaway and his wife, yes, I did hear something about them. I'm sorry, naturally, but I really don't see where I come into the picture at all. If you suspect that there has been foul play of some kind, surely the police are the people to contact.'

She made to get to her feet. 'Besides, I'm going to be extremely busy this morning. I have several appointments, with the lawyer and one of the contractors who is carrying out work for me on the manor.'

'Please sit down,' said Fenner quietly. 'That's one of the things we've come to talk with you about.'

She hesitated for a moment, then sat down staring moodily in front of her. Her lips were drooped into a petulant curve and there seemed to be no life in her eyes. Fenner felt a tiny shiver pass through him as he looked at her face.

She was no coward, he felt certain of that. Previously only a day or so earlier, she had been a charming, vivacious woman, bubbling over with enthusiasm for the job she was having carried out. Now she was changed completely in a few short hours. Something had got into her; but he wasn't sure what it could have been.

'What is it you want to talk about?' she asked icily. 'Please make it brief. I have a lot to do this morning.'

'You know that Mrs. Kennaway died during the night and that we have fears for her husband's sanity?'

'I heard something like that,' she admitted. 'Where do I come into it?'

'I think you'll remember that a few days ago, we warned you against tampering with things you knew nothing about, But you chose to ignore our warnings and went ahead with your plans for the manor. You still intend to live there when

140

it's finished, I suppose?'

'Naturally. I've had my mind set on this for almost twenty years and nothing is going to prevent me now.'

'I was afraid of that,' muttered Chambers. He stirred uneasily in his chair. 'I ought to have considered the possibility, of course, but — '

'What on earth are you talking about?' snapped the girl. Her voice was like a whip crack in the room and Fenner thought he detected a vicious quality about it which he would never have suspected from the pleasant, tough, determined girl he had known before. What under the sun could have changed her so in such a short time? Had that place up there been having this effect on her?

'Miss de Ruys,' Fenner leaned forward in his chair, 'Can't we discuss this thing like civilised people? You seem to have got it into your head that the only reason why we're trying to dissuade you from going through with your plans is that we don't want you here in the village. Nothing could be further from the truth.'

'I'm afraid that I don't believe you. Doctor Fenner,' she said bitterly. 'Ever since I came here, you've been against me. None of the people in the village would work for me, even though I offered them almost twice as much as I'm paying the town people at the moment.'

'That isn't the reason at all,' persisted Chambers. 'We're fighting evil here — not you. You're merely instrumental in bringing the evil to a head. Look upon yourself as a magnet, if you wish, that can attract all of this evil. If you continue as you are doing, you'll become the focal point for it, concentrating it, so that no one will be able to fight against it. When that happens, God help everyone in this village.'

'Do you think I care what happens to your village?' muttered the girl viciously. 'Once I take over the manor, I'll be mistress here, just as my ancestors were the masters of the whole area. They had the power and they knew how to use it.'

There was an expression of horror on the older man's face and even Fenner could not prevent himself from staring at her in stunned surprise. This wasn't the Angela de Ruys he had known a few days earlier. This was someone entirely different. Someone — *evil*.

'What's got into you?' he asked tightly. 'You've changed completely the past two days.'

'Have I? Perhaps I've only just come to my senses. Perhaps, ever since the others died in the manor, time has been standing still up there, waiting for this very moment. I've felt it myself whenever I've been there, the sense that very soon, there will be a fulfilment of all that the house has been waiting for and that this waiting across centuries will not have been in vain.' A thrill of ecstasy filled her voice, but it was a sound that sent shivers of ice down Fenner's spine.

'Can you tell us what has made you so different?' Chambers asked.

'What do you want me to say? This is something far too big for me to be able to explain it to you. If you don't know by now, then you never will.'

She paused, then glanced at both of them in turn, her eyes bright.

'I suppose you know that both of you will be destroyed before many more days have passed?'

Fenner stared at her incredulously, although Chambers did not seem to be unduly surprised, almost as though he had considered this a possibility.

Her smile broadened viciously. She got to her feet. 'I think you'd better go now,' she said harshly. 'If you want my advice, keep away from the manor, at any time. Prying into things like this won't help you.'

With an effort, Fenner got to his feet, and stood waiting for Chambers to get to his feet, then moved towards the door. They had done everything they could have. But at least, they had a rough idea of what they were up against. If only he could understand what had got into the girl, what had changed her to this degree.

At the door, he paused and looked back. 'You're making a big mistake, you know,' he said sickly.

'I think I'm quite capable of looking after myself, Doctor,' she said confidently. 'It's you who ought to be careful. You wouldn't understand me, I suppose, if I told you just how helpless and powerless you are. Dabbling in these things which you don't understand.'

'I think I understand only too well,' Chambers answered. 'But perhaps we're not entirely as helpless as you think we are.'

'Are you? I wonder!' She laughed thinly and the sound was still ringing in Fenner's ears as they went outside into the chill sunlight.

'Where do we go from here, Paul? There's nothing more we can do here, is there?'

'On the contrary, there's quite a lot we can do, but we'll need very careful preparation. Thank God you asked me to come along to see her, John. Even now, we may not be too late.'

'Too late?' Fenner looked at the other in surprise.

'I suspected it the moment we entered the room. Didn't you see the way she winced when I said that I hoped she'd give up her idea, otherwise only God could help everyone in the village?'

'No, I didn't. But what would that mean?'

'To me it could only mean one thing. Something has taken over possession of her. That's the only way they can make her go through with her plans. I'm more convinced than ever that she is to be the central figure in this fiendish drama. She's merely a puppet with these inhuman creatures pulling the strings.'

Fenner looked at him in horrified fascination. 'Are you sure of this?'

'Quite sure. The only way we can fight these creatures now, is through her. She's to be the focal point for whatever diabolical witchcraft they're perpetrating. We foiled them once with the Sussamma Ritual. It may not help the next time. But at least we can be prepared. First we must drive this unclean thing from her mind. Then we may be able to get at the truth. Drastic measures may be necessary and I'll need you to help me. But you mustn't be surprised or shocked at anything you see or hear.'

7

Dark Revelation

'Somehow, I don't care exactly how you do it, you've got to get Angela de Ruys here. Once you've done that, I'll take over. I'll need you here but this ought to be straightforward, provided they haven't had time to take a tight hold over her mind.'

'Very well. I'll do my best. But I only hope to God you know what you're doing.' Fenner sipped his drink slowly. 'What do you intend to do assuming I succeed in getting her here?'

'No ordinary doctor — no disrespect, John — could do anything for her in her present condition. I know something of the ritual for ridding someone of these elementals that can take possession of souls. If we're successful, we can bring her back to her normal state of mind, and also learn something of these creatures.

147

Even though we get rid of the force that is motivating her at the moment, she will still retain some of the memories in her subconscious. In order to get at them, I'll have to use a light hypnosis.'

'I'll do what I can to get her here,' Fenner said grimly, 'even if I have to use force.' He glanced at his watch. 'She's probably up at that devilish place now She said she had to see the contractors this morning. I'll go up there on the off-chance of catching her. It may give me the opportunity of bringing her back in the car without arousing her suspicions. I'll drive her straight here if everything goes according to plan. Give me an hour or so.'

'I'll see to it that everything is ready for you when you arrive,' promised the other. 'Just one word of warning, however. Be very careful yourself while you're there. The workmen may be safe enough. They don't count for anything in this issue. But I'd wear this if I were you. It'll afford you some measure of protection.'

He handed over the small golden crucifix on its slender chain. 'Wear it around your neck for every single minute,' he said gravely. 'They may try to do everything in their power to get you to take it off, even to the extent of making it feel as though the chain is biting into your throat, choking you. Resist it and the feeling will pass, I promise you.'

'I'll remember that.' Fenner nodded, took the crucifix and slipped it around his neck. The metal felt cold against his skin.

Outside, he walked quickly to his own house, got the car out of the garage and drove up the hillside to the manor on the top. As he drove he noticed that although it had started out clear and sunny at the bottom, the closer he got to the top of the hill, the foggier it became. His fingers gripped the wheel tightly and he bit his lower lip as he leaned forward over the wheel, peering into the white wall that seemed to have been thrown up around him. He had the chilling sensation that the fog, or mist, whatever it was, was actually following him, moving with him, rather than his moving into it.

If only he could see where he was going. The car bumped and lurched over the rough, stony ground. There were deep gullies on either side of the half-obliterated road, which he knew from past experience, but in this damned fog it was impossible to see them at all. He was driving blindly. For all he knew, he was going round in circles moving further and further from the old road, toward the rocky ledges of the hillside, where there were almost precipitous drops of several hundred feet. If he once went over the side there, it would be the end of him.

The note of the straining engine roared in his ears as he drove more slowly.

Then, almost as suddenly as it had come, the fog began to clear. It drifted away swiftly in writhing tendrils as if possessing some fiendish life of its own, or as if it being torn to shreds by invisible plucking fingers.

Directly in front of him, lay the manor, tall crenellated towers stretching up towards the sky. There were men working there on the site and the sound of hammers and saws reached him the moment the mist drifted away. He had deviated a short distance from the road, but somehow, some hidden Providence had kept him away from the edge where it dropped steeply from the hillside.

Stopping the car in front of the manor, he switched off the engine and climbed out. There was no sign of Angela de Ruys, but it was possible that she was inside. One of the workmen eyed him curiously as he approached.

'Could you tell me if I could find Miss de Ruys on the site,' he asked, stopping the other.

The man glared at him sullenly and, for a moment, Fenner thought that he would refuse to answer. Then the man jerked his thumb behind him.

'You'll find her in there with the boss,' he said shortly. 'Is she expecting you?'

'I doubt it,' Fenner said, trying to force cheerfulness into his voice. 'But it's important that I should see her as soon as possible.'

The other moved aside, blocking his path as though to prevent him. For a moment, Fenner glanced down at the heavy shovel that the other held in his hands, swinging it loosely, menacingly. A tiny stab of fear passed through him. Were all of the men on the site affected in the same way? Did working here for even such a short space of time, have this effect on anyone? It might be the answer to what had happened to Angela herself. Could it be that Chambers was being a little too pessimistic and seeing evil elementals where none really existed?

He stared the other in the eye and a moment later, the man started back, then stood to one side, to let him pass. Glancing down, Fenner saw that the neck of his coat had fallen open and the bright sunlight was glinting brilliantly on the crucifix.

Inside, there was activity and orderly confusion. On the face of it, it could have been just another construction and repair job. But on closer inspection, he noticed the men did not seem to be working normally. Their eyes were dull and glazed and their movements too puppet-like and automatic, as though they were being directed by something outside of themselves, by some extraneous force that kept them going when they would willingly have thrown down their tools and stopped.

He noticed too, how cold it was inside the house. There seemed to be a kind of deadness about the place. As if he were standing in the wings, watching a puppet show, with some invisible puppet-master pulling the strings, jerking them every few moments, keeping the men at their individual jobs, hurrying them, making them finish more quickly than they would normally have done.

He looked about him swiftly. There was no sign of Angela in that room and he walked quickly through towards the rear of the house. A moment later, he saw her. She had her back to him and was in deep conversation with one of the men.

He waited until she had finished speaking and the other had moved away, before going forward.

'Angela.' He spoke quietly, but she whirled instantly, her face a frozen mask of surprise and instinctive wariness.

'Why did you come here?' she demanded angrily. 'Have you come to spy on me now?'

'Nothing of the kind,' he said quickly. 'I merely came to see for myself how the work was progressing. If you won't stop this, then we must accept the position as it is.'

She seemed to relent a little at that, but the wary expression was still there in her eyes and she watched him narrowly.

'I'm glad you're seeing things my way, Doctor.' Her voice had softened a little, but it didn't fool him. She was still highly suspicious of him and somehow he had to prevent that suspicion from becoming magnified in her mind.

He shrugged indifferently. 'This is your place,' he said calmly. 'No one can dispute that fact. You're perfectly entitled to live here if you wish, I suppose. Although personally, it isn't the kind of place I'd like to stay in myself. What are you going to do for servants? Surely you won't be able to remain here by yourself. It's far too large a place.'

'I hadn't given that much thought,' she admitted. 'But I suppose I ought to be able to get people to come here and live in, if the money is right. I know I won't get anyone from the village. They're all far too set in their foolish ways regarding this place. Not even the fact that it has been altered will change their minds, I suppose. Still, I ought to be able to engage some from the town. They can't all be as superstitious as the people around here.'

'Maybe they're superstitious for a very good reason,' he said quietly.

He saw the brief anger flare at the back of her eyes and wondered whether he had gone too far.

'All right, Doctor, so there are a good many tales going around the countryside all relating to the manor. It's a great pity, I think, that you and your friend don't do a little more to squash these idle rumours rather than indulging in them yourselves. I might feel a little more kindly disposed towards you if that were the case.'

'I think I understand your point of view,' he said evenly. 'But if you had seen those things we witnessed last night, I think you might have been able to understand ours. Don't you feel the coldness in this place?'

'It's only because we're out of the sun. There's no heating in yet. Once I get the central heating units installed, you'll find a tremendous difference.

'How long do you estimate before it's all complete and you're ready to move in?'

'I don't know exactly. Perhaps another three or four weeks.'

Fenner nodded and followed her around the house while she explained the various points to him, but he found it significant that she never once took him to the back of the house, into that room with the queer cabalistic designs painted on the floor under that dusty carpet; the room which looked out over that decaying, half-forgotten graveyard where all that was earthly of the terrible de Ruys family, lay under the soil.

Twenty minutes later, when they had finished their tour, he said: 'If you want to get back into the village, I've my car outside, I could give you a lift. It would save all that walk down the hill.'

'Is that the reason why you came here?' she asked him quickly.

He shook his head, trying to keep his face expressionless. 'Certainly not,' he lied. 'I didn't even know that you were here when I came. But since you are here and you've taken all this trouble showing me around, I think the least I can do is offer you a lift back.'

She hesitated, then nodded her head. 'Very well then. But I'll have to go straight to the hotel. I still have quite a lot to do before lunch.'

'I'll take you straight there,' he promised, leading the way out of the manor. Compared with the deathly cold inside the building, the wan sunlight seemed almost like summer. Once inside the car, he let in the clutch and they started off slowly down the hillside. Fenner peered ahead of him, trying to see the fog which had plagued him during the ascent, but the air was completely clear now. He could see the individual houses in the village clustering at the bottom of the hill, and one or two people walking in the street.

Reaching the edge of the village, Fenner swung the car expertly along the main street. He could sense a certain tension in the girl, but as yet, there was no hint of suspicion on her features as she stared directly ahead.

Now came the tricky bit, he thought tightly. There were still one or two people on the pavements and if she tried to stop the car, or get out of it while it was still moving, she would cause quite a scene. Theoretically, he could be arrested for attempted abduction if she cared to press the charge, and in her present mood and condition, he didn't doubt that she would do so, particularly if she guessed what he and Chambers were trying to do.

At the corner, he swung the wheel quickly. There was a thin screech of protest from the tyres.

The girl caught at his arm, pulling it sharply. 'Where are you taking me?' she demanded harshly. 'This isn't the way to the hotel — and you know it!'

'I'm sorry I had to do things this way, but Paul Chambers wants to see you urgently. I was sent to bring you — by force if necessary.'

Suddenly the girl twisted violently in

her seat and tugged at the door with all of her strength. Savagely, he chopped down on her wrist with his free hand and she fell back into the seat with a startled cry of anger and pain.

'Sorry I had to do that,' he said softly. 'Chambers will explain everything when you meet him.'

'Both of you are stupid fools!' She spat the words out savagely. 'You don't know what it is you're doing. They will take a terrible revenge. You can't even begin to guess at the strength of this dark force you're trying to fight. If you could then you would soon leave it alone, before it destroys you.'

'I wouldn't be too sure of that,' said Fenner firmly. 'Chambers knows far more about these things than you obviously give him credit for.'

He was saved from the necessity of any further explanation as they arrived in front of the house. He stopped the car and looked across at the girl. The narrow lane was absolutely deserted apart from themselves as he got out of the car and held the door open.

'If you're thinking of trying to run away,' he said warningly, 'I assure you that you wouldn't get very far and I won't hesitate to use force to take you in there.'

'Terrible retribution will fall on you both for what you're trying to do,' she said as he led the way into the house.

Chambers opened the door for them, motioned them inside. He gave the girl a quick, speculative glance then nodded to Fenner: 'I didn't expect you to be so successful. Did they make any attempt to prevent you from getting back?'

'There was nothing on the way back, but, on the way there I ran into the thickest fog I've ever seen in my life. It seemed to cling to me as I neared the top of the hill. Then, just as suddenly, it vanished.'

'One of the lesser manifestations,' Chambers said. 'Fortunately, it was daylight, and the crucifix would help. Now, if you'll bring Miss de Ruys through into the other room, everything is ready.'

He gestured towards the half open door. Fenner took Angela's arm and led her forward. She went unresisting, but

160

just inside the open doorway, she paused as she saw what lay in front of her and a terrible, bubbling shriek rose up in her throat. Beneath his fingers, Fenner felt the muscles of her arm knot and writhe as she struggled to move back.

The carpet had been turned back and weird designs had been drawn upon the woodwork of the floor. Triangles and pentagons had been inscribed inside large, intersecting circles. Small glass phials had been placed at the corners of the figures and each of these, he saw, was filled with a clear liquid. At intervals around the circles, candles had been placed in slender silver sticks. They were unlit as yet.

'Keep a tight hold of her, John, for God's sake. Her reactions prove that she has been possessed. Don't be afraid you'll hurt her. It won't be Angela who'll feel it, but the creature inside her.'

Fenner tightened his grip on the girl, half-dragged her into the room. Chambers closed the door and locked it behind him.

'Now we'll begin,' he said tensely.

'Bring her over here.'

There was a faint sneer on the girl's face as he led her forward, but she did not attempt to resist him now. Chambers came towards her. There was a look on his face that Fenner had never seen before. A look of rapt, intense concentration. His lips were moving silently as he traced the sign of the cross in front of her. Instantly, she writhed and fought like a wild animal with short, savage grunts coming from between her lips. The look on her face was terrible to see. It took all of Fenner's strength to hold her still. Then, as suddenly as it had begun, the spasm passed. He saw to his astonishment that she was in some form of trance, her eyes staring glassily in front of her, the lines of her face fixed and set as though carved from marble.

'Place her in the centre of the pentagram,' said Chambers soberly. He waited until Fenner had picked her up and laid her down on the floor, then he lit the candles in the silver sticks.

The smoke that came from them was sharp and pungent. Fenner prevented

162

himself from coughing with an effort and stood back, watching the other closely.

'We have to take all of these rather elaborate precautions,' Chambers said, 'in the event of the elemental materialising. Then it will be confined inside the circle and cannot get through to us.'

Fenner nodded, although he understood little of what the other was talking about. He kept his eyes fixed on the slender body lying inside the ring of candles and crystal glass containers, watching the girl with a curious expectancy.

Something began to happen. At first, the effect was so slight, so faint, as to be scarcely noticeable.

A kind of mist seemed to be rising from the girl's mouth spiralling upward where it mingled momentarily with the smoke from the candles. Then it thickened, grew stronger and denser, seeming to take shape in front of his eyes.

The smoke from the candles was little more than a faint haze, but the mist that now lay over the girl's inert body had taken on shape. An ugly, fearsome shape which leered at them from the confines of the circles which seemed to gather itself to strike, lunging forward, then pausing as if it had struck something invisible, a barrier past which it could not go.

Fenner had recoiled instinctively at that sudden thrusting lunge. Then he recovered himself. This was what Chambers had warned him about. The elemental.

Horrible and squat with wide, leering features, it hovered there in the air on a level with his eyes, glaring at them with a look of thwarted malice in the red eyes. For a moment, it took on the features of the long-dead Henry de Ruys as they had seen him before. Then the shape changed again in fleeting, rapid succession. It was man, it was woman, it was beast and devil. Fenner felt his mind reel and was scarcely aware of the fact that Chambers, standing beside him, was muttering something under his breath, making strange signs in the air with the fingers of his right hand. The very air inside the room seemed charged with electricity as the battle of the two powers continued. Sweat was pouring down the other's face, but not once did his lips stop moving, not once did he halt in his endless chant.

Then, quite suddenly, there was a scream of fiendish rage, a high-pitched sound that raced along Fenner's nerves, threatening to unbalance his mind. It was a sound of pure evil that seemed to hang in the air long after the twisted, writhing shape had flowed inward upon itself and gradually vanished inside the circle.

'It's gone,' said Chambers, his voice drained of all its usual energy. He went over to one of the chairs in the corner of the room and sank down into it.

Fenner crossed over to him. There was nothing more to fear from the girl or the thing that had been inside the circles. He knew that instinctively. It was Chambers who needed immediate attention now.

He poured the other a glass of brandy and held it to his lips, making him sip it slowly, until some of the colour came back into his face. His grey hair was plastered close to his scalp with sweat and his hands were shaking a little.

'I'm all right now,' he said huskily, a moment later, and sat up. 'How is she?'

'Still the same,' said Fenner. 'But that thing inside the circle has gone.'

'Good. I doubt whether it will come back. It may, but not at the moment. Now we must carry through the second part of the experiment.'

'The second part? But I thought that was all you intended to do.'

Chambers got slowly to his feet. 'You forget that now she is under my influence, I must question her. The memory of what had happened will still be in her subconscious. If I can dig it out, we'll know what those evil things are doing. We may even be able to throw her mind right back, through time, while she's under hypnosis.'

'But can that be done?' There was a note of incredulity in the younger man's voice. 'I know that some people, under hypnosis have given accounts of things which have happened to them, reputed to be in earlier lives and this has been put forward as a strong case for reincarnation. But frankly, I've never believed in the validity of these experiments. Most of them have been conducted by known charlatans.'

'True. But in this case, we're working with something a little different. She is of the same family as those evil, grave-spawned things we saw in the manor grounds last night. Not only that, but for them to have possessed her, she must have been en rapport with them. That's the strongest type of affinity one can possibly have. I think we'll find that we can get her to talk of things which happened even three centuries ago.'

Chambers walked over to the outer circle drawn on the floor. The candles still burned in the slender sticks, but there seemed to be less smoke from them than before and there was not the same sickly smell at the back of their nostrils.

'Angela de Ruys,' said Chambers softly.

'Yes.' The voice was faint and far away, and Fenner could have sworn that the girl's lips did not move in the waxen face.

'Can you hear what I am saying?'

'I can hear you.'

'Good.' A sigh of relief escaped from the other's lips as he went on: 'I want you to answer all of my questions ... no matter what they may be. You understand?'

'I understand. What is it you wish to know?' It seemed odd and incredible that the thin voice could issue forth from the girl's mouth without her lips or a single muscle of her face moving at all. It was as if something else inside her were speaking the words, something crouched inside the shell of her body, obeying the other's commands. For a moment, Fenner thought that it might be the elemental, still there, lying in wait. But one glance at his companion's face was enough to convince him that this was not the case.

'You've been controlled by an evil entity for some time now. Do you know who — or what — it was?'

'Yes. It was Henry de Ruys.'

'Then he's not dead?'

A pause, then: 'Not as you know death. His body died, but not his soul. That still lives on, earth-bound because he wished it that way, because he sought immortality and that is the only way possible for mortals to gain immortality.'

'I see.' Chambers licked dry lips. Beads

168

of sweat still glittered on his forehead. 'What is Henry de Ruys doing now? Do you know?'

'Trying to reach through to you. But it is still daylight and his power is not sufficient, either to reach you, or to break through the circle around me. He wants me to stop telling you this, to stop answering your questions.'

'Where is he now?'

'In the grave where he has to stay during the daytime. Only at night, can he take shape and wander at will.'

Chambers said quietly: 'Now I'm going to take you back, right back to the days before you were born, to the time three hundred years ago before Henry de Ruys died.'

8

The Witchcraft Rites

Fenner stood tensed in one corner of the room while Chambers questioned the still, unconscious figure of the girl, surrounded by the burning candles.

The swirling mist had gone completely and he was able to see every detail of her face, the still, unmoving lips and the open eyes that stared straight up at the ceiling above her.

'You're going back now, far back through time, one hundred, two hundred, three hundred and fifteen years. What do you see?'

'I see a small room with strange symbols drawn on the floor. There is a single window looking out over the garden at the back of the house.'

'Which house is it?' snapped Chambers harshly.

'The manor — on top of the hill.

Mendringham is down below us, two miles away.'

'Go on. Try not to omit any details. What is happening there?'

'They are waiting for someone. Five of them — waiting.'

'Five!' Almost savagely, Chambers said: 'You are now in the body of Margaret de Ruys. Quickly — tell me who the others are in the room beside yourself and why you are waiting there.'

To Fenner's amazement, the voice suddenly altered. The whole character was different and he could have sworn that it was another woman in the room with them, speaking the words:

'We're waiting here for my father. My mother is standing by the window looking out into the garden. My brothers Martyn, James and Edmund are also with us. This is to be the culmination of everything we have worked for all these years. Very soon, my father will come and bring with him what we need for this to be a success. If it works this time, we shall all be immortal. He has promised us that. Only Edmund is afraid. He has always been afraid

171

whenever we have done this. Sometimes, I think he does not want to be immortal, but like the other stupid people in the village, who are content to live and die like animals. In fact, they are no better than animals, any of them. That is why we use them for our work.'

Fenner shivered at the tone of the voice. It seemed to drip malevolent hatred.

'Go on. What is happening now?'

'I can hear a noise outside. My father must be coming. Yes — it is he. I can see him quite clearly now through the window, coming along the garden path. The man with him seems drunk. Perhaps that was the easiest way to get him here. None of the villagers will come near us now. They shun the place and with good reason.'

The voice broke off into a horrid, cackling laugh that rang through the room, grating on Fenner's raw nerves.

'Jump forward half an hour,' commanded Chambers. 'What is taking place now?'

'Edmund has gone. He fled as soon as

Father came into the house. It seems he wants no part of the immortality that will soon be ours. Father says that we are to let him go. I saw him running headlong down the garden path a few moments ago. He may have fallen over the edge and been dashed to pieces on the rocks below. If he has, perhaps that would be judgment on him for doing this. But the rest of us are ready for the sacrifice to begin.'

'Sacrifice!' In spite of himself, Fenner could not keep back the word.

'Quiet!' warned Chambers. 'We're coming to it now. Don't move or speak again.'

Fenner nodded tautly. The other turned back to the girl in the centre of the room. 'Now listen carefully, Margaret de Ruys,' he said loudly. 'I want you to tell us everything that happens. This is important. Do not leave out a single detail. You understand?'

'I understand.' There seemed to be a certain reluctance in the voice now. It was as if some power were struggling with Chambers to take over control again, to break the slender hypnotic thread that bound them to the past. Several of the candles too, had almost burned to the bottom. Very soon, they would gutter and go out.

The voice floated eerily from somewhere in the middle of the circle. Fenner listened entranced as it spoke of terrible obscenities, of the sacrifice that had been committed in that room at the back of the manor, all those years before, of how the terrible de Ruys family had sought for, and found, a kind of immortality. Some of the words made no sense to him, but Chambers seemed to understand them, for he kept nodding his head.

'The sacrifice is ended. The Great Master has been pleased to accept it from us. There can be no doubt now that we have succeeded after so long.' There was triumph in the voice, but it was fading swiftly now as though being drawn away by some unseen power.

'Just forward three weeks. What do you see now?'

'It is strange. I thought that there would be only darkness and a feeling of unbeing. But instead, there is a power flowing through me that I never knew before. I can move at will. I can see but objects are dim and hazy. There was pain, terrible pain when they burst into the house and searched through the rooms until they found us. The man we used was missed and they finally plucked up the courage to take the law into their own hands. They were frightened. Oh, I can still sense the fear in them when they came into the house.' A trace of delighted ecstasy touched the fading voice.

'They took our bodies away and thrust stakes through our hearts but by that time, there was nothing they could do to us. The pain was soon over and after that there was freedom such as we had never known before. Edmund was a fool not to have shared this with us.'

'What do you mean by freedom?' demanded Chambers. One of the candles on the far side of the circle flickered and threatened to go out. He spoke quickly and intently, as if realising that he was fighting against time now.

'Freedom from the limitations of our earthly bodies, of course. What else? The Great Master kept his promise. He said that we should never die. Now we shall be here forever until another of the family comes to claim this place. Then we shall have the power denied to us even yet. The power to return to the flesh, because then we shall — '

The far away candle gave one quick flicker, then went out. In that same instant, the voice stopped as though sheared through by a knife. The silence was complete and final.

Chambers sighed. 'We'll learn nothing more today,' he said in a tired voice. 'But at least, we know more than before.'

'We know what happened to Edmund,' said Fenner grimly. 'So that's how it happened.'

He watched as the other walked around the circle, snuffing out the candles individually, lifting the tiny glass phials, careful not to spill a single drop of the liquid they contained. Then he went over to the girl, made the sign of the Cross over her once more, muttered something under his breath and took hold of her hand.

Her eyes flickered open. For a moment, they stared straight ahead and Fenner saw that there was no memory, no recognition in them. Then she sat up and gradually, the old light came back into her eyes and face.

'Why, Doctor Fenner,' she said softly. 'And Mr. Chambers. What am I doing here?' She looked about her in mild surprise, trying to take everything in.

'It's too long a thing to explain right now,' said Chambers gently. 'Let's say that you've been suffering from temporary loss of memory. You're all right now though, I promise you that.'

'Is that true, Doctor?' She turned to look at Fenner and he felt a strange catch in his throat as her gaze fell on him. He nodded slowly.

'That's right, Angela,' he said quietly. 'Just take it easy for an hour or so, and try not to worry over things which you don't remember. Perhaps they're best forgotten anyway.'

'I'm not sure that I understand what

you mean,' she said hesitantly, 'but you're the doctor. I suppose I have to do what you say.'

'Of course you do,' he replied banteringly. He began to feel a little easier in his mind. They were still in danger, he could feel that, but he had the idea that, perhaps even now at the eleventh hour, they were winning through.

But then another thought struck him and the chill returned to his mind. What would happen once the sun set and the darkness spread over the countryside, cloaking the manor on top of the hill and bringing the bats in their silent hordes from the black ruins of the old church nearby? When dead things that could not rest, walked the earth and madness was abroad.

Would Chambers prove to be the most powerful then, or would that evil thing take over Angela's mind once more, this time never to let go until it had achieved its vile purpose?

The girl sat in one of the chairs and took the drink that Chambers offered to her. She glanced down with a faint touch of horror on her features at the cabalistic designs on the floor and a little shudder went through them. Her eyes were troubled as she looked up at Fenner.

'Something has happened,' she said in a low voice. 'Something evil and terrible, if you had to go to these lengths to help me.'

Fenner said: 'We don't want to bring you into this unholy business if we can possibly help it, Angela. It's best if you can be kept out of it altogether.' He looked across at Chambers as he spoke, his face almost pleading.

The other shook his head. 'I'm afraid we couldn't do that no matter how much we wanted to,' he said thickly. 'Do you think I want to drag her into this mess, John? Unfortunately, we have no choice. I've a feeling that things are coming to a head in the very near future. If we're to stand any chance at all, we must be prepared for them. Above all, we must prevent them from getting Angela here into their hands again.'

He took the girl's hands in his own and went on; 'At the moment, I'm not sure what your role in this business is, but it's something extremely important. They mean to use you for some rites they have in mind.'

He got swiftly to his feet and paced up and down the small room.

'But these people of whom you speak have been dead for over three hundred years,' protested the girl.

'They aren't dead as we know death,' Fenner explained slowly. 'I'm not sure just what they are. Call them earth-bound spirits if you like. They meddled with Black Magic just before they died and the final culmination of their evil rites was human sacrifice.'

'Human sacrifice!' There was genuine horror in the girl's voice. 'But why should — '

'They wanted immortality — and they got it apparently, but not in the way they thought. The terrible evil associated with them is still there, crystallised inside that place. No matter how much you alter it, you can't destroy that. And we have reason to believe that through you, they'll somehow be able to materialise, to assume flesh and blood.'

'But is that possible?'

'Who knows? There are so many aspects of this evil business that it's impossible to be positive about anything. It could be done, I suppose, but it would require a tremendous concentration of power, of evil vibrations, to bring it about. Even then, I wouldn't like to forecast how long this materialisation would last.

'Of one thing I am certain. If they do succeed with their plan, you will never survive. I don't want to frighten you unnecessarily, but it's vital to keep you away from them, where they cannot get at you again.'

'You mean you don't want me to go near the manor until this is all over?' Angela asked.

'I mean much more than that. They will try again after dark when their strength is far more potent. You could be almost anywhere and they could still reach you.'

'Then there's nowhere I can hide?'

'I didn't say that I said they could reach you *almost* anywhere. For example, you would be quite safe inside one of these circles. If we could obtain some of the Sacred Host, you would be perfectly safe anywhere on this Earth. But I'm afraid that is out of the question. We would need a special dispensation for that and I'm not sure whether we could find a priest who would grant it at such short notice.'

'Then she must remain here during the day and when night comes, we must make a circle and she can sleep inside it,' declared Fenner harshly.

'It's not that simple,' Chambers said. 'We have both been without sleep for most of last night and part of the previous night. It's certain that one of us would fall asleep, if not because of sheer exhaustion, because of the fiendish power these creatures possess and then the ring would be broken.'

'So we're lost,' said the girl hopelessly.

'Don't give up so easily,' said Fenner quickly. He took her hand. 'I'm convinced that, with Paul's knowledge, we'll beat them yet.'

She smiled wearily and her slim fingers tightened in his.

'I know you're lying to help me,' she said softly, and there was something in her eyes that brought a catch to his throat. 'But I'm deeply grateful.'

Fenner got to his feet. 'Is there nothing we can do to fight them?' he demanded bitterly.

Chambers shrugged. 'We'll take all of the precautions we possibly can,' he assured him. 'We have the Powers of Light on our side. They are immeasurably stronger than the others if we can only summon them to our aid.'

'Will that be difficult?' asked Angela.

'Well . . . ' Chambers was non-committal. 'It won't be easy.'

★ ★ ★

Twenty minutes later, the telephone rang. Fenner lifted it from the cradle. Sergeant Weldon was on the other end of the line. He sounded agitated.

'That you, Doctor?' he asked hurriedly. 'Is Chambers there too?'

'That's right. Do you want to speak to him?'

'No. You'll do for what I've got to say, Doctor. It's something right outside my experience. I don't understand it at all.'

Fenner took a tight grip on himself. He sensed that some fresh horror was about to break.

'That man they buried up at the cemetery a few weeks ago — Pendrake. Somebody has rifled the grave! I think you and Mr. Chambers ought to come along and take a look at it — see what you think about it. Frankly the whole thing has got me puzzled.'

'All right. We'll be right out.'

'Fine.' There was undisguised relief in the other's voice. 'I'll meet you out there.'

Fenner laid the phone back in its cradle like a man in a trance.

'What was it?' asked Chambers tersely. 'Sounded like bad news to me.'

As Fenner hesitated, the girl said sharply: 'Something's happened, hasn't it?'

Fenner spoke dully. 'The Sergeant says that somebody has been up during the night and tried to rob Pendrake's grave in the cemetery. He wants us to go up there right away. He'll be waiting for us when we get there.'

Chambers shrugged. 'Very well. We'll have to go.' He threw a swift glance at the girl. 'I don't know what kind of experience this is going to be, but I think, for your own safety, you ought to come with us. I'm not going to let you out of my sight for a single instant.'

'You think something might happen to me while you're away — even in broad daylight?'

'It's possible this may be some kind of trick,' said the other fiercely. 'It may have been some creature imitating Weldon's voice. Or even if it was him, he may not have been speaking of his own volition.'

Chambers went to one of the drawers at the side of the room, took out something, and handed it to the girl. 'I think you'd better wear this around your neck. It will afford you some protection at least.'

She took the crucifix and slipped it over her head and around her neck. Chambers nodded. 'I think we're ready now,' he said grimly. 'Your car outside John?'

The other nodded. 'It won't take long to get out there,' he said confidently. 'And if anybody tries to stop us on the way, anyone in the least suspicious, I swear I'll drive right over them.'

They went outside, Chambers carefully locking the door behind him. Five minutes later, they had left the village behind and were driving along the road leading to the isolated cemetery. The road was virtually deserted, with only a few cars and trucks moving in the opposite direction.

Fenner swung the car into the cemetery, passing through the iron gate and on to the broad strip of gravel road which wound its way around the perimeter of the burial place, making a full circuit of the graves.

A moment later, they spotted the small group of men standing around the new grave on the far side of the ground. It was impossible to mistake the tall, burly figure of the police Sergeant even from that distance.

He stopped the car a few yards from the little group around the grave and got out, holding the door open for the others. They made their way across the hard, frosty ground to where Sergeant Weldon stood waiting.

'Glad you could come, both of you,' he said quietly, giving Angela a curious glance. 'This is something you might be able to explain, Paul. I'm quite sure that I can't.'

Chambers moved forward and the little group of men stood apart to allow him to pass through. Fenner followed close on his heels.

'Oh my God!' The words seemed to have been jerked from the older man's lips.

Swiftly, Fenner moved forward until he was peering down over the other's shoulder. At first, all he could see was the upheaval of the soil where it had been moved away from the grave.

Then, he saw what had brought on the other's involuntary exclamation. With a tremendous effort, he found his own voice:

'That hole. It's been dug up from the inside, from underneath the ground!'

For a brief, wild moment, his world threatened to collapse around him. His stomach felt as if it had suddenly jumped up into his chest, as if he had gone down in a sudden fast elevator.

'You see now why I decided to call you, Paul,' said the Sergeant. 'How can you possibly explain this?'

'I think we'd better dig down and see what we find at the bottom,' suggested Chambers tightly. 'Do your men have shovels with them?'

'Certainly. I had them bring them along just in case. But don't you think this is a case for the coroner?'

'Strictly speaking — yes. But I'm afraid we haven't time for formalities at the moment. I'll take the full responsibility if anything happens.'

Weldon was immediately officious. He spoke to the men standing by and a moment later, albeit somewhat reluctantly, they began to dig. For some strange reason, the soil did not seem quite as hard there as it was underfoot and they made rapid progress. Fenner watched from a few yards away, almost as though he were fearful of what the men might find once they dug down to where the coffin ought to have been.

He could feel the girl trembling beside him. 'What do you think they'll find, John?' she asked tightly.

'I don't know,' he answered, 'but we should find out soon. Another couple of feet and they'll locate the coffin.'

Moments later, the spade struck something which was not soil, which echoed hollowly as the workman made another thrust at it with the spade. He looked up from the depths of the hole, inquiringly.

'Dig it out and bring it up here where we can take a look at it,' ordered Weldon tersely. 'But be careful.'

The soft earth was scraped away from around the coffin. From where he stood it was impossible for Fenner to look down into the hole to the very bottom and although he heard the startled gasp and the sudden cry from the men down below, it was impossible for him to see the cause. Then the Sergeant stepped forward and passed down the strong rope to the men below. In the sunlight, Fenner could see that his face was white and beaded with sweat. He looked like a man who had just seen a ghost and even Chambers, standing on the very edge of the grave, looked sick around the gills.

'What's happened down there?' whispered the girl.

'I'm not sure.' He held her back, afraid himself of what they might see. His heart was fluttering uncomfortably in his chest as the men on top began to haul on the ropes, bringing up the coffin from below.

Slowly, it came up and he could hear it banging against the earthen sides of the grave. Then it came into view, swung for a moment before the Sergeant and one of the watching men reached out and hauled it on to the ground at the side.

Fenner sucked in his breath in a startled gasp. The wooden lid of the coffin had been smashed and splintered as though by a giant's fist. The thick wood had been shattered like matchwood by some savage blow.

A blow that had been dealt from inside the coffin!

9

The Dark Power

For several moments, there was a shocked silence among the small group by the graveside.

'Did you expect anything like this to happen, Paul?' said Weldon after a while.

'Never in the whole of my life.' He lifted his head like a man in a trance and stared at Fenner. 'He was dead, of course. There could be no doubt about that?'

Even though he had expected a question like that, Fenner still felt shocked by the suggestion. 'He was dead all right when we put him in that coffin. I'll stake my life on that.'

'Then how the devil do you explain this?' The police sergeant waved a hand to embrace the scene in front of them.

'I can't explain it. Not at the moment,' said Chambers. 'But I have a feeling that we shall know the answer very soon.

Tonight, perhaps.'

Weldon blinked rapidly. 'You're not suggesting that a dead man suddenly took it into his head to batter the lid off his coffin and dug his way out of that grave, are you?'

'I'm not suggesting anything at the moment, Sergeant,' muttered Chambers thickly. 'But if you can offer any better explanation of the facts as you see them there, then I shall be extremely glad to hear it.'

'Dead men don't just get out of their coffins and roam the countryside. That belongs to the old days of witchcraft and superstition when people didn't know any better.'

Chambers smiled tightly. 'Perhaps when they knew a little more than we do now. Sometimes, I wonder if we haven't grown a little too clever with all of our scientific principles and gadgets. Maybe there are forces far more basic than any of these.'

'Black Magic?'

'Perhaps . . . I don't think there is anything useful we can do here, Sergeant.

If you like, you can get the men to bury that coffin and cover it completely. There's no reason why this should be spread through the village, although I doubt whether these men will be able to keep this to themselves for long. It's the kind of secret that can lead to madness if kept.'

'I think I see what you mean, Paul.' The other turned and gave an order to the men standing around the graveside. They looked at him curiously, then did as they were told, touching the coffin with looks of revulsion on their faces. There was fear in their eyes too, Fenner noticed.

Fear of the unknown — of the evil shapes that had been seen occasionally among the bleak moors on the northern edge of the village by those returning late at night from the nearby towns and villages.

By afternoon, it would be all over the village. Women would bolt and shutter their doors and windows, keep their children off the streets after dark; as if that would stop them, he thought tensely. Locked doors and shutters meant little to them when they were abroad.

There was the soft clunk of earth hitting something wooden and solid as they walked towards the car. It reminded Fenner of the day, several weeks earlier, when they had laid the earthly remains of Pendrake in the ground. Then they had thought that it would all be finished as far as he was concerned. Now, they had discovered to their horror that it had only been the beginning.

He shivered as he slipped behind the wheel and pressed the starter. The engine coughed once, then burst into uproarious life.

He was glad when they drove out of the woods and came on to the open stretch of road before the village. He felt tired, pleasantly drowsy. It was difficult to remember when he had last had a good night's sleep. It seemed such a long time ago.

His eyes lidded. There was a sudden warning shout from Chambers sitting beside him as the other reached out and grabbed the wheel. The action jerked him fully awake. They were almost off the side of the road.

'I don't know what came over me,' he said thickly. 'I must have fallen asleep over the wheel. God, that's something I've never done in my life before.'

'Are you sure you're all right, that you can drive the rest of the way?'

'Certainly. I'm perfectly all right now.' He edged the car back on to the road.

Fifteen minutes later, they were back in the room with the weird designs painted on the floor.

'In the light of what's happened,' said Chambers, 'I think it would be best if you both remained here, not only for the rest of the day but during the night too. We'll take it in turn to sleep during the afternoon. Once it's dark, it's imperative that we should all be wide awake. That's important.'

The rest of the day passed uneventfully. They slept for two hours and kept watch for two hours. Angela was not included in this arrangement and slept most of the time, waking shortly before six o'clock to find the other two men both awake. Chambers went out of the room and returned a few moments later with three cups of hot, black coffee on a tray.

'We may need a lot more of this before dawn,' he said firmly. 'Fortunately, it's something I always keep. It helps me to stay awake whenever I have a manuscript to finish.'

The hot liquid scalded the back of Fenner's throat as he gulped it down. But it had the effect of driving all thought of sleep from his mind as he settled himself down in the chair in front of the blazing fire in the wide hearth.

'You think they'll try again tonight?' asked the girl suddenly, breaking the uneasy silence.

'Yes, I do,' Chambers nodded. 'I'm practically certain of it. Once we took you out of their hands, it meant that they had to do something drastic. That's why they forced Pendrake to break out of the coffin.'

'Then he isn't really dead.' Angela shuddered as she tried to forget what she had seen earlier that day in the isolated cemetery.

Chambers grimaced. 'Oh, he's dead, all right. Make no mistake about that.'

'Then how — '

'I'm afraid,' went on the older man gently, taking her arm and leading her back to the chair, 'that you don't understand what it is we're fighting. We aren't fighting things of flesh and blood and the powers they can command aren't things that we can examine scientifically. These are the dark things, the black knowledge of evil that has been sought throughout the long ages, but discovered only by a few. All of the knowledge that has been gained is there for you to read and study if only you know where to look for it.'

Chambers checked his watch, then walked over to the window, twitched aside the heavy curtains for a moment, and peered out, his brow puckered in thought. Over his shoulder, Fenner could see that the moon had risen, round and full. It shone with a dull reddish tinge, very similar to the harvest moon. But at this time of year, that colour seemed odd and unreal, strangely out of place.

Outlined against it, every detail clearly visible, he saw the tall, sky-rearing building on the hill. The moon was directly behind it, a great gleaming ball, lining the walls and turrets with its glaring light. He shivered. Ordinarily, he regarded the moon as something benign and friendly. Now there was terror in it and fear. It was something grotesque and abnormal, a vast red eye that watched them unwinkingly from the starlit heavens.

Then the other had pulled the thick curtains back into place and the illusion vanished. There was a coldness on his face that even the heat from the blazing fire could not remove. His legs and arms felt numb and strange, as though they were no longer a part of him.

'I think we'd better prepare ourselves,' said Chambers quietly. 'It's dark now. Very soon, things may begin to happen. And with Pendrake out there somewhere, probably up at that accursed place already, waiting to play whatever part they have for him, we will need every ounce of strength and determination we can summon up.'

'I'm ready,' said Fenner grimly.

'Good. I need you to help me get the pentacle ready. It won't take us long. After last night, everything is ready to put into place. But we must hurry. There may be little time.'

Fenner followed the other's directions, although it was difficult for him to understand half of what he did. The broad chalk lines were drawn over those that had been painted earlier. For some odd reason, the paint seemed to have faded until in places it was almost non-existent. The five-pointed star was finally drawn to Chambers's satisfaction. Then the strange cabalistic signs were drawn on the floor, the small bunches of asafoetida grass were placed in position to seal the room as far as possible from anything which might attempt to get inside.

Eventually, just as the clock in the village was striking seven, everything was complete. Chambers straightened his back and glanced about him.

'I think, just to be on the safe side, we ought to remain inside the circle during the night. I've no idea when or how the attack will develop, but we ought to be ready for it. Remember, both of you, that whatever happens, you are not to set foot outside of the circle. So long as you remain inside you are safe from whatever comes. Outside, and you could be destroyed in a single instant.'

'We understand,' said Fenner. He took the girl's hand and together, they stepped over the wide chalk line that glowed with a dull light on the floor, inside the middle of the circle. Chambers followed them. He deliberately left the lights on in the room and the fire had been heaped up so that it was blazing fiercely, sending out waves of warmth to every corner of the room. It would continue to burn like that for hours.

'That's better,' said Chambers, with a faint sigh. He settled himself with his back to the others, and motioned them to do likewise. 'This is so that we can watch in all directions,' he explained. 'If you see anything happen, whatever it might be. Don't get up or try to turn away from it. Just tell me what you see and I'll know what to do.'

The tall, tapered candles set at the corners of the five-pointed star burned steadily, their flames blue in the harsh light of the three bulbs set close to the ceiling. There was no draught in the room and they scarcely flickered. Fenner found his gaze jerking swiftly from one corner of the room to the other. A tense silence settled. Outside, there was the faint sound of the wind in the branches of the large tree which grew tall and straight near the window and occasionally one of the branches would scrape against the glass, the sound sending little tremors up and down Fenner's spine.

Half an hour passed. Then an hour. In the distance, the clock chimed again, the sound carrying clearly on the frosty air. Even through the curtain. Fenner could plainly see the huge shape of the moon as it rose higher into the sky. It seemed blurred and distorted by the curtain, like a ball of fire hanging suspended in the void.

Nothing seemed to be happening. More and more, he felt a growing sense of scepticism in his mind. He wanted to leap to his feet, to tell Chambers that he was through with this childish stupidity and that he was going home to be where he would, at least, be able to get some much-needed sleep; and to sleep in peace without all of this weird Mumbo Jumbo.

He was on the point of rising angrily to his feet when he remembered what the other had said, that the attack might be directed against them in subtle ways. This must be one of them, and he hadn't realised it. He gritted his teeth and listened to the sound of the wind soughing around the house with low moaning sounds. Gradually, the feeling of scepticism went away and he felt more at ease.

'What time is it now?' asked the girl quietly, breaking the silence.

A pause, then Chambers said calmly: 'A little after eight-fifteen.'

'Nothing seems to be happening.' said Fenner, without turning his head. 'Maybe — ' he paused uncertainly.

There was a faint scratching at the door. The sound was so sudden and unexpected that he winced physically and his flesh began to crawl.

'What on earth was that?' The girl's frightened whisper reached him a second later.

'Just keep your heads. Stay calm.' muttered Chambers warningly. 'This may be it!'

The scratching was repeated several times, sometimes near the bottom of the door, but more frighteningly, sometimes near the top as though the creature, whatever it was, had lifted itself up on its hind legs and was rearing up there in the darkness only a few yards away with only the wooden door between them.

Faintly, Fenner could hear the ticking of the grandfather clock in the outer room, above the scratching at the door. Then, after what seemed an eternity, the sound ceased.

The minutes ticked away. Once Fenner glanced down at his watch, and was surprised to find how slowly the time had gone. It seemed like hours since Chambers had said that it was only around eight-fifteen, and yet only thirteen minutes had passed since then. He lifted his watch to his ear. It was still ticking normally.

The shadows in the corner of the room began to lengthen. At first, he scarcely noticed them. Then he jerked himself upright, sure at last. The fire in the hearth spluttered and began to die away as though water was being poured upon it by some invisible hand.

The warmth faded too and a draught of cold air blew across his shoulders. He glanced at the window curtains, but they were hanging limp and unmoving.

'Something's going to happen, Paul. There's a cold draught coming from somewhere close at hand and the fire seems to be going down.'

'That's what I expected. Don't be afraid of anything you might see. They'll try to scare us first before they pit their real strength against us. Hoping to make us step outside of the circle.'

'Don't worry, Paul,' Fenner said. 'I don't intend to move from this spot.'

'Good. And if anything does materialise, try to pray. Nothing complicated because you'll be sure to forget the words.

Simply repeat over and over again, in as loud a voice as you can 'Lord protect us'.'

The fire in the hearth sank lower and lower. Even the light from the electric bulbs close to the ceiling seemed dimmer than before. The flame of one of the candles flickered convulsively as the cold, icy draught played on it insidiously.

Something shrieked wildly and shrilly immediately outside the window. He felt Angela jerk against his back, heard the sharp scream as she turned her head. Something dark and monstrous, its true shape ill-defined but giving the impression of horror, appeared for a brief moment at the window, just visible where the moonlight threw its shadow on the curtains,

'Ignore it,' muttered Chambers warningly.

Fenner sank back, sitting down again. Almost unwittingly, he had stepped close to the edge of the circle.

He began praying under his breath. Behind him, the girl was repeating the words over and over again in a loud clear voice which trembled slightly at times, but which nevertheless carried to the four corners of the room.

Was it only his imagination, wondered Fenner, or had the lights brightened slightly once the girl had begun to pray? And the fire too seemed to be burning in the hearth with a renewed vigour.

He heard Chambers sigh with relief, but he knew better than to turn his head to look in the direction of his friend. The lurking fear in the corner of the room had merely retreated, it had not gone altogether. Rather it seemed to be gathering itself for a fresh onslaught against them. He kept his eyes glued to the spot where he had last seen it.

The girl was still speaking, but her words seemed slurred and twisted, as if she were falling asleep, trying to say them.

The shadow thickened, took a vague, ill-defined shape, crouched in the corner. He could see the wall through it vaguely. Then it seemed to gel. The features became more distinct. Seconds later, he found himself staring into the red, hate-filled eyes of Henry de Ruys.

With an effort, he found his voice, said

hoarsely: 'It's here, Paul. Crouched there in the corner. The same as we saw at the manor. That abomination which calls itself Henry de Ruys.'

The shadow skittered around the room, flicking from one point to another so that it was almost impossible to follow it. The fiendish chuckle of pure malice and hatred lifted the hairs on his scalp, stretched his nerves almost to breaking point.

He grew aware that Chambers was muttering vague phrases under his breath in a low, monotone. The words were some that Fenner had never heard before.

The shadow retreated a little, but the red eyes still remained fixed on Fenner's face, glaring at him with an oddly hypnotic quality. He wanted to get up out of that ring of chalk. He wanted to move out and strike that hateful face. He knew that if only he could get his hands around the scrawny, scraggy throat, he could choke what little life there was left out of that abomination.

Almost before he was aware of it, he was scrambling savagely to his feet. He scarcely heard the older man's shouted warning.

'For God's sake, John, stay where you are. This is only a trick to get you out of the ring.' With seconds to spare, his words penetrated Fenner's confused brain. He sank back and there was a look of thwarted fury on the face that glared at him from the corner of the room.

A quarter of an hour later, although he was not sure exactly when, the thing vanished. The lights in the room brightened and the fire flared up swiftly in the hearth. Warmth came back into their bodies and the cold, chill air went away.

'They've realised that it won't be easy to defeat us.' Chambers spoke quietly and confidently from somewhere at Fenner's back. 'But we haven't finished yet. There'll be more to come.'

Apart from their quiet breathing and the faint ticking of the clock in the outer room, the house was completely silent. Even the wind outside had died away entirely and the occasional tapping of the branches against the windowpane seemed to have stopped completely. The moon, too, was no longer visible through the curtain over the window. He guessed that it must be almost midnight, but he could not be bothered to look at his watch. There would be nothing they could do until dawn except sit and wait.

The room was warm now after the chilliness that had pervaded it a few moments before. At least, he thought tensely, we'll have some warning of an impending attack. Always, the temperature had dropped whenever they were being assailed by these powers of darkness.

He stifled a yawn. The room was becoming uncomfortably warm now. He moved his legs slowly, careful not to extend them so that any part of them went over the chalked circle. The flames on the tall, slender candles burned brightly and steadily. There was no trace of evil in the room now, he felt certain of that. If there came any, he felt reasonably sure that he would recognise it instantly and be ready to meet it.

He half-smiled to himself. He was becoming almost as adept as Chambers now at recognising these things. It seemed ludicrous, though, he reflected that he, a doctor of medicine, a man devoted to curing people of their physical ills, should find himself here, in this room, squatting inside a pentangle, with candles burning at the points, waiting for evil to materialise.

His right hand moved lazily to his jacket pocket. The flat, heavy shape of the revolver was still there and he knew that it was fully loaded. He would not hesitate to use it if anything came into the room through either the door or the window. A little trickle of amusement drifted through his mind. How the devil did you kill a ghost, a man who had been dead for three hundred years? Certainly not with a gun and bullets.

'Do you think we've stopped them for good, Paul?' he asked finally.

There was no answer. It seemed that the other must have fallen asleep. Without moving, he spoke the girl's name softly. Still no answer. Everything was very, very quiet.

Oh well, he thought, there can't be

much to be afraid of now, if the others have gone to sleep. May as well make myself as comfortable as I can if I have to spend the rest of the night on this hard floor.

He settled himself down, clasping his hands tightly around his knees, drawing them up against his chest. The fire spluttered and blazed in the hearth.

Very likely, Paul had said something about sleeping in turn, and he had been so engrossed in his own thoughts that he had not heard him; or if he had, the fact had not registered.

He glanced at his watch. A little after ten o'clock. He'd give Paul until eleven, then wake him for his turn at watch. No sense in waking Angela, she needed all the sleep she could get, poor kid.

He shifted his feet once more. He wasn't sleepy at all, he told himself fiercely, but his eyes kept lidding and closing, lidding and closing, and his head kept jerking forward on to his chest.

Behind him, the fire brightened for a moment, then began to dim. Only the red wires of the bulbs near the ceiling glowed.

The shadows stretched themselves out from the corner of the room. Something scratched insistently at the door, wanting to be let in. At the window, a loathsome shape appeared.

But John Fenner was sound asleep and none of these things woke him or impressed themselves upon his consciousness.

10

The Undead

John Fenner woke with a start. His body felt cold, his limbs numbed. His arms and legs moved stiffly as he stretched himself and stared about him. In the dim light, he managed to make out the bookcase pushed hard against the wall in front of him and the carpet rolled back against it and memory returned with a rush. He had slept even when Paul had warned him against it.

The fire in the hearth had dwindled into ashes and only a pale glow remained. The candles had burned themselves out. Afraid, startled, he glanced at his watch. It was almost three-thirty. Something had happened, he felt certain of that. Swiftly, he turned his head, careful of where he placed his feet, although he had the odd sinking feeling that whatever evil was to happen that night, had already happened and there was no longer any need for the protective circle.

Paul Chambers was still lying there with his head on one arm, his eyes closed, breathing slowly and evenly. But there was no sign of Angela de Ruys.

Cursing bitterly, Fenner shook the other roughly, savagely, by the shoulder.

Paul's eyes flicked open a moment later and he turned his head to stare up at the other. For a moment, there seemed to be scarcely any recognition in his gaze. Then he sat bolt upright looking about him.

'Angela! She's gone,' said Fenner savagely. 'We must have slept some time during the night. I remember shouting to you, but neither of you answered so I decided to stay awake myself. I must have fallen asleep too. When I woke, a few moments ago, she had gone. The candles had gone out too.'

'That's what I feared.' The other pulled himself to his feet. 'They must have come once they'd lulled us into a false state of security and lured her out of the ring. It wouldn't have been difficult for them. If they could put us to sleep as simply as that, getting her out of the protective circle would have been child's play for them.'

'But where is she now? What the devil have they done to her?'

'Steady, John. I know how you feel. But we must proceed carefully. Once we step out of the circle, they may attack us and I doubt whether my power would be enough to save us if they did attack us then.'

'But why should they? For God's sake, Paul, they've got her. That's all they wanted!'

Ignoring the other's restraining hand, he stepped over the chalked circle into the room. Nothing happened. There seemed to be no attempt to control his mind and a moment later, Chambers did likewise. They stood together for the moment, looking down at the drawing on the floor that had failed to protect them.

'Almost certainly they've taken her to the manor,' said Fenner. He pulled the gun from his pocket, checked it mechanically, then slipped it back again. 'I'm

215

going up there. Are you coming with me?'

'Of course I'm coming,' muttered the other tensely. 'Though I doubt whether that gun will be any protection.'

'I'll get my car,' Fenner said as they went outside, into the cold, clear, frosty night.

Paul shook his head. 'You'd stand no chance at all of finding your way up there in the car. It will be quicker for us if we walk it.'

'Very well, if you say so,' Fenner agreed reluctantly. Together they made their way between the rows of quiet, slumbering houses, out to the edge of the village. The moon hung low in the west now, throwing a pale yellow light over the surrounding countryside.

At first, they made good progress but gradually, the strain began to tell on both of them. Fenner forced his flagging muscles to obey his will, but the other was tiring visibly. The country grew more wild and snaking roots and bushes seemed to thrust themselves up out of the ground underfoot, clutching at their legs and feet at every turn. On occasions, a wild animal jumped across their path, skittering away into the moon-thrown shadows around the trees.

Fenner could visualise all sorts of gruesome, hideous things lurking in the tangled undergrowth, ready to launch themselves out of the shadows at them. There seemed to be far more narrow, steep-sided glens cut in the side of the hill as they toiled up the steep slope than Fenner remembered. Each of them was filled with midnight shadows where the trees seemed to slope fantastically up towards the moonlit sky. Even the clouds that occasionally passed over the face of the moon had an oddly distorted colour and appearance.

They reached the point where the old road all but vanished into coarse scrub and brush. More than half a mile further on, the manor stood atop the hill, looking down at them.

Over everything there seemed to be an odd haze of curious restlessness. Nothing seemed to be still although there was no wind. Branches swayed on the trees and an occasional bat flew low over their heads, silhouetted momentarily, grotesquely, against the moon. Fenner hurried as quickly as he dared, taking the other's arm and almost dragging him forward. The ground was treacherous in many places.

Their breath was coming in quick, harsh gasps now and both were panting and sweating with the exertion. It seemed impossible that they could go on until they reached the very brow of the hill.

Whatever had taken the girl had got a very good start on them. They stood little chance of getting her back from these creatures before they had begun their devilish ceremonies, and if Paul was right, she would be dead once those rites had been concluded.

They reached a bend in the track. Ahead of them the ground stretched bare and desolate until it curved over the brow of the hill and levelled off where the manor stood. The topmost walls of the large building were just visible from where they stood, but the rest of the place was hidden by the rocky lip of the hill. No lights showed in the place even. The manor brooded sombrely in the night, dark and silent, but not empty. Of that Fenner felt sure.

The thought of what might be happening there, especially in that terrible room at the back with the cabalistic signs on the floor, urged him on. He moved forward, then turned swiftly. The other was still standing where he had left him.

'Come on for God's sake, Paul,' he hissed. 'Every second is precious now.'

'Quiet! There was something there a moment ago. I saw it.'

'Where?' Fenner retraced his steps.

'Straight ahead — about forty yards away. It moved out into the open for a second.'

'Could you see what it was?'

'Not definitely. But it reminded me of what we saw when Kennaway was taken away.'

'Oh God!' They went forward, striving to move more quickly now.

Then, before they had progressed more than twenty yards, they saw it clearly as it crossed a patch of moonlight. A loping, brutish shape that carried the inert figure of the girl in its arms.

The next instant, they were almost swept off their feet by the howling gale that came roaring down the hillside. The wind tore and plucked at their clothing, battering their tired, weary bodies, threatening to pick them up bodily and hurl them back down the hillside, down to death and destruction at the bottom.

Grimly, Fenner forced his way forward. His grip on the other's arm tightened automatically. Slowly, step by step, they stumbled forward, heads down. The weight of fifteen invisible men seemed to press down upon them as the gale shrieked and screamed about them.

Fenner risked lifting his head to peer into the darkness ahead. The dark, shambling figure they had seen a few moments earlier had vanished without trace.

After a timeless period, they reached the end of the track where it ran through the tall stone gates, the clawing pillars surmounted by the winged daemons striving to touch the lowering clouds.

The house loomed high in front of

them, dark and forbidding. There was something immeasurably more evil about the place now. The sense of fear had been there before when they had last visited it together, but now that feeling, that chill sensation of impending disaster had multiplied itself a hundredfold in Fenner's mind.

He pulled himself together with an effort.

'They must be inside this very minute,' he said loudly, raising his voice to make himself heard above the howling of the wind.

'We've got to go inside,' he said tensely, taking the other's arm. 'Angela is in there with those fiends.'

By now, the clouds had completely covered the moon and it was pitch black. There was a vivid flash of lightning as they made their way forward over the rough ground that bordered the drive. The peal of thunder, when it came a few moments later, seemed to shake the hill and rock the house in front of them to its very foundations.

Then the storm burst about them with

all its savage fury. Rain slashed down in glancing sheets, beating against their eyes and faces.

Ten yards further on, Chambers suddenly stumbled over something that lay in his path and went down on to his knees with a faint cry. Fenner hurried forward as the other picked himself up slowly. Then he uttered a sharp exclamation as he saw the figure lying in the rain-slashed mud.

'It's Angela!' he shouted.

Swiftly, Fenner felt for the pulse. There was another brief flash of brilliant lightning that lit up everything. He saw the girl's face etched clearly, whitely, in front of him. Her eyes were closed and the rain was running down her cheeks. There was a smudge of dirt on her forehead. Several tense seconds fled before he detected the pulse, faint and irregular, beneath his finger.

'She's alive, thank God,' he said harshly. 'She's alive! Do you think they had any chance to carry out their devilish tricks with her?'

'I don't think so. If that was her we saw

on the hill, they wouldn't have had time to complete any elaborate ceremony.'

'Why have they left her here?'

'I'm not sure. This may just be a manifestation, and not Angela at all, something put here to delay us while they carry out their rites inside.'

'But it is her!' protested the other.

'I sincerely hope so.' The other fumbled in his pocket, brought out a tiny knot of garlic flowers and the crucifix. He placed the garlic on her brows and the cross on her still lips.

There was no movement of the features. She lay as still as death and only the faint beat of the pulse told him that she was not dead.

'It's Angela all right,' he said hoarsely. 'But why should they leave her here for us to find when they need her so badly?'

'Who cares so long as she is here,' muttered Fenner. 'Now let's get out of here and take her with us. Once we're clear of this place we should be able to bring her round.'

'No, John.' Paul laid a restraining hand on his arm. 'This is serious — there's something else at the back of all this. They may have found someone else, someone whose presence at their rites is even more powerful than Angela's. After all, she is merely one of the family. Possibly they look upon her as a reincarnation of one of that terrible quintet, I'm not sure. But there is one other who can prove an even more potent tool in their hands.'

Fenner looked at him aghast. 'Who might that be?' he asked tensely.

'The Undead,' said Chambers in a taut whisper. Even above the howling of the wind, his voice carried to Fenner. 'Pendrake. The Undead. Brought back from the grave. That way, they had two chances. If we managed to stop Angela, then they still had him.'

'And you think he's in there now? That they're going through with the Black Mass or something like it, while we're out here, delayed with Angela?'

'I'm sure of it. Remember what that old woman raved about before she died.'

'About the shapes that seemed to be everywhere?'

'Not only that. Remember how she said it was difficult to get away from this place. That there always seemed to be something calling to her, some lost voice, drawing her back, even against her will.'

'I remember. What of it?'

'I think that must be what happened to Pendrake. Even though he was dead, it still had the power to bring him back to this place. I wonder how often that poor devil wanted to get away while he was still alive and yet he couldn't do so. Maybe he was glad to die because then, he figured he would escape it. Yet even dead, he couldn't.'

Fenner looked towards the silent house and felt the fear settle over him, chilling his mind and body.

'Is there no way to stop them?' Hope was dying swiftly inside him. The elation he had felt on finding Angela alive and apparently unharmed was dissipating swiftly.

'There might just be a chance,' the other was saying. 'But it's a desperate one and I'm afraid I'd only be a hindrance inside there. That climb has taken almost all of the strength from my body.'

'Just tell me what to do and I'll go in there,' muttered Fenner impulsively. He got to his feet. 'You stay here and watch over Angela.'

'You'd be taking a terrible risk, John. If they have performed their secret rites, then you will be lost. Nothing could save you.'

'I'm prepared to risk that. Now, quickly, what must I do?'

'Destroy them by fire. Burn down the entire building with them in it, while they're away from the remains of their earthly bodies inside the coffins.'

'Fire, but — '

'There will be an oxy-acetylene lamp around left by the workmen, and plenty of fuel for the compressors.'

'Of course,' Fenner nodded. He threw one swift glance at the girl lying so still and silent on the rain-soaked ground, then walked swiftly towards the manor which seemed to be waiting for him to enter.

The rain was still lashing down in torrents as he pushed open the wide front doors and stepped inside into darkness, and the foul, indefinable stench of the grave. *They were here*, screamed the little warning voice at the back of his mind. *They were in this place, hiding in the shadows that lurked everywhere, waiting for him.*

He deliberately left the wide doors open. There was no telling when he would have to return and in a hurry. Away from the full fury of the storm outside, he glanced about him. Nothing moved and only the hollow ringing echoes of his own footsteps accompanied him as he made his way cautiously through the clinging darkness.

There was no telling where they were, although the most likely place was undoubtedly that small room at the back, overlooking the unhallowed graves.

He searched the lower floor of the building and discovered where the workmen kept their drums of fuel oil and the oxy-acetylene torches. If possible, he would have to surround these fiends completely with fire, so that it was impossible for them to pass around it.

That meant he would have to go into that room.

He worked swiftly and steadily, driven on almost beyond the limits of human endurance by the urgency of what he had to do. Everything, it seemed, depended upon him now. By the time he had soaked the floor in the fuel, and emptied the contents of a second over the stairs, he could sense the feeling of evil growing stronger.

He made his way towards the tiny room at the rear of the house. The sickly, nauseating stench of the grave was there, stronger than ever, cloying his nostrils, making him want to retch. Even the sharp, aromatic smell of the fuel with which he liberally soaked the walls and floor could not destroy it.

By the time the second drum was empty the place had been almost completely soaked in the highly inflammable liquid. All it needed was the spark to ignite it.

A door opened somewhere in the near distance. He heard the eerie creak of rusty hinges and felt the cold draught on his body a second later. Desperately, he fumbled with the oxy-acetylene welding tool, but his fingers seemed to have no feeling left in them and refused to do what he wanted them to do.

A moment later, he heard a dry chuckle from the darkness in front of him. The room in front of him, beyond the doorway began to glow with a fiendish light all its own. By it, he could make out the five figures standing watching him with baleful eyes.

He knew that he had to turn and run, but his feet refused to move. The evil laughter rang out again and this time it was joined by other voices, until the echoes shrieked and chased each other through the long corridors of the house. The thunder answered the screams of insane laughter. The whole house seemed to shake.

He knew then that he was lost. There could be no escape from this place for him. Whether or not they had finally completed their rites, he did not know. But the fact remained that he could not move a single muscle of his body to ignite the fuel-soaked floor and walls.

Lips moving soundlessly, he tried to pray. He could feel the sweat pouring down his face and the muscles of his arms and legs jerked convulsively without his control. His entire will was concentrated in the attempt to hurl himself backward, away from these terrible creatures of the night, yet except for the muscle twitching in his face, his body was held completely motionless by those waves of satanic power which emanated from the room, pouring out through the open door.

Then, beyond the five dark figures that stood watching him, he saw something else move, almost at the very edge of his vision. A stumbling, jerking figure that seemed to have no control over its limbs, like a dead man trying to walk. The realisation came to him in a single flash of understanding. Pendrake! The Undead. Forced back by these fiends for their own devilish purposes.

He watched, tensed, as the dead body walked forward impelled by some hidden motive. What the other intended to do, Fenner could not guess.

But there was something in the other's hand, something that he held furtively but with a singleness of purpose that was evident in every line of his body. There was a brief flash of sparks from the dark object. Then something struck the floor in front of the dark creatures that watched him from the doorway.

Fenner was not sure what happened after that. There was a savage blast of brightness and flame of searing heat that singed his face. Then he could use his limbs again and fear and terror urged him back, through the leaping, roaring flames, back to the open doors. His lungs were bursting with the smoke and his eyes were blinded so that he could scarcely see and he was forced to find his way out of the blazing inferno by touch. How he made it he was never sure. It seemed there must have been some Providence guiding him.

The next thing he remembered clearly was Chambers dragging him away through the teeming rain that felt blessedly cool and refreshing on his upturned face. Somewhere, there was the sharp crackling of flames and a bright red glow, which seemed to spread up from the ground, up, up to the base of the clouds themselves, lighting the whole area.

'It's all over now,' said Chambers softly. 'They're finished. Now and for ever. You succeeded.'

He shook his head, grew aware that Angela was sitting up, watching him with a faint smile on her lips. 'I failed,' he said softly. 'It was Pendrake in there who paid his last debt to society.'

There was a quiet understanding in Paul Chambers's eyes as he nodded. They walked slowly down the quiet hillside, in the moonlight, the storm blown away and the crumbling walls of the manor behind them engulfed in belching flame and smoke.

THE END

We do hope that you have enjoyed reading this large print book.

Did you know that all of our titles are available for purchase?

We publish a wide range of high quality large print books including:
Romances, Mysteries, Classics
General Fiction
Non Fiction and Westerns

Special interest titles available in large print are:
The Little Oxford Dictionary
Music Book, Song Book
Hymn Book, Service Book

Also available from us courtesy of Oxford University Press:
Young Readers' Dictionary
(large print edition)
Young Readers' Thesaurus
(large print edition)

For further information or a free brochure, please contact us at:
Ulverscroft Large Print Books Ltd.,
The Green, Bradgate Road, Anstey,
Leicester, LE7 7FU, England.
Tel: (00 44) **0116 236 4325**
Fax: (00 44) **0116 234 0205**

Other titles in the
Linford Mystery Library:

RAT RUN

Frederick Nolan

Her Majesty's Secret Service agent Garrett, investigating a series of suicides by scientific researchers, discovers the parameters of a cataclysmic terrorist strike. The fanatical André Dur puts his unholy scenario into operation over the geological fault called the 'Rat Run', where nuclear submarines stalk each other in the dark depths. Helplessly the world looks on as the minutes tick away. Garrett's desperate mission is to neutralise Dur's deadly countdown — the ultimate ecological disaster, Chernobyl on the high seas.